TRYLONS AND PERISPHERES

Short Stories

Also by Roger Lee Kenvin

After the Silver Age

The Cantabrigian Rowing Society's
Saturday Night Bash

Harpo's Garden

The Gaffer and Seven Fables

Krishnalight

TRYLONS AND PERISPHERES

Short stories

by

Roger Lee Kenvin

JULY BLUE PRESS

Published by July Blue Press, 126 Mt. Cardigan Road, Alexandria, New Hampshire, 03222   jlybl@earthlink.net

First printing 1999

Printed in the United States of America by Odyssey Press Inc., Dover, New Hampshire

Library of Congress Catalog Card Number: 98-75524

ISBN 0-9656635-4-X

ACKNOWLEDGMENT

"Mama Bannerjee Riding on a Peacock," originally appeared in *Potpourri*; "The Sadhu of Faizabad Road" in *Reflect*; "Wedding Night in Jaipur" in *India Currents*; "Viajes Autobus Azul" in *The Secret Alameda*; "Castlemartyr" in *Garm Lu: A Canadian Celtic Arts Journal* (Canada); "The Goodbyes" in *Explorer*; "Trylons and Perispheres" in *The Villager*; "Parachute" in *Green's Magazine* (Canada); "The Day after the Earthquake" in *The Crescent Review*; "The Last Major Appearance of Baker Tompkins" in *S.L.U.G. fest*; "Finding Mickey Rourke" in *Breakfast All Day* (England); "The Promotion Committee" in *Inlet*.

For the people in the photograph:
James Marion Kenvin, Ivy Macdonald,
and William White Mitchell

"What is a photograph a photograph is a sight and a sight is always a sight of something."

Gertrude Stein

CONTENTS

MAMA BANNERJEE RIDING
ON A PEACOCK

The three dachshunds are yowling. The mali stiffens in the rose garden. Rahat glides slowly out the door from the main house and disappears toward the kitchen, his separate and private province under the Indian sun. There is a commotion along the polished verandah.

Mama Bannerjee arrives, a pirate ship in full sail, with her three children in tow.

"Mr. Wales," she says as I meet her at the entrance to my apartment in the house. "We are just stopping by to collect you."

"Oh?"

"We are going to make our puja. Have you forgotten? You are to be coming with us."

"I had," I confess. "I'm sorry."

"Today is Basant Panchmi. We are due at the Union. I knew you would be most put out if we didn't stop for you." Her eyes are great reflecting pools of passion and feeling. Her smile is brilliant, disarming. "You see, I am most careful to insure that your Indian education is complete."

We are out the door now. Rahat is standing in the doorway of his kitchen looking apprehensively at us. "We shall be at the Chand Bagh Union," I tell him. "We'll be back in time for tea."

Rahat nods assent, but when Mama and her brood turn their backs to him and walk down the polished verandah toward their rickshaw, he sticks out his tongue at her like a surly child. Only I see this. I laugh. Muslim against Hindu, but they get along, usually.

"What is so amusing?" asks Mama Bannerjee. "It is the first day of spring, according to our Hindu calendar. I have already bathed and fasted and made my private puja. Now, you must go with us to this more festive one."

Mama has commandeered two rickshaws. She orders her children, Ranjan, Avril, and Kum-Kum into one, and puts me into the other with her. "We shall run a race," she declares. "Hazratgunch," she orders the driver and indicates that she wants the hood pulled down on the rickshaw. Mama loves to fly through town with interesting people beside her. She loves to flaunt her independence and cosmopolitanism to all her provincial neighbors. I am honored to be her prize trophy for today.

Mama Bannerjee is someone I have known for about a year since I came to India to work on my dissertation at the university. She knows that I am interested in Hinduism and descends upon my bachelor household whenever something unusual comes up that she thinks the great American scholar should know.

She leans over toward me and whispers confidentially, as though the rickshaw driver, who speaks no English, might understand: "Basant Panchmi is a spring festival, especially dedicated to young virgins."

The other rickshaw passes us at just this moment. I look longingly at Avril, an extraordinarily beautiful young woman of eighteen whom I am in love with. Mama follows the direction of my eye. She laughs. Nothing is lost to her. Do I detect approval of the direction of my glance?

Mama presses on: "All the young virgins wear green and yellow saris, the colors of spring."

The other rickshaw pulls ahead of us, Avril in green, laughing back at us, Ranjan, egging on the driver in race-horse fashion, and Kum-Kum, a petulant young mango of a sister, scrunching down for fear of flying dust.

"This puja will intrigue you, I know," Mama says to me. "All the young people come and worship at the feet of the goddess of wisdom, Saraswati, who, on this day, represents especially music, dancing, the graceful fine arts."

"Is it a sort of fertility rite?" I ask.

Mama laughs heartily. "Naturally," is all she says at first. Then she falls silent, but erupts into laughter again. "All our religion is some form of fertility rite," she adds.

We pull up in front of the huge red sandstone building, the Union. I offer to pay the rickshaw driver, but Mama waves aside my attempt, saying, "No, no. You are my guest. Let me pay." She gives the driver only forty-five naya paise, and then wafts up the stairs with her children in her capacious wake, I trailing. The driver holds out a begging hand to me and turns on pleading eyes. I give him some more coins. It bothers me that Mama mixes charm with callousness so glibly.

At the top of the stairs Mama is waiting. She has divined what I have done. "It is not good to spoil them," she scowls. "Now, remove your shoes here."

I do so, and then Mama takes my arm and leads me into a large room, fragrant of sandelwood. There is a shrine of the goddess Saraswati set up at one end, with lotus petals strewn on the floor and chalk-paste marks describing floral designs.

"Saraswati is usually depicted riding on a peacock, as you are aware," Mama whispers to me. "But today she is all in white for virginal innocence. In her hand she carries a sitar. Behind her, you will notice that great peacock circle of spring colors. Naturally, her statue is raised higher than us because all our gods must always be taller than the worshippers. Our heads should just be reaching the level of the god's feet."

Mama moves over closer to her children. "Today," she proclaims, "Saraswati is being prayed to by all those students who have been told by their parents that if they fulfill their religious obligations to the goddess--fasting and making puja--they will pass their university examinations coming up in a month." Mama touches her handsome son Ranjan on the shoulder. He is taking a master's degree in English literature. "If they don't pass their examination," Mama whispers portentously, "Watch out."

A priest moves out now and stands directly in front of us. He makes the *namaste* gesture and we do the same. The priest is accompanied by a muscular young man in a bright orange tee-shirt who offers us little saucers made of jungle leaves.

"Fruits of the springtime," coaches Mama.
"Take one."

I do. I recognize a gooseberry, banana slice, and a little sugar-paste candy in it. I pop it into my mouth. It has an unusual taste, like a Bengali sweet.

Later, over tea back at my place, Mama discusses education.

"Mr. Wales, you have your degree from Harvard University," Mama says to me. "What do you think of this nonsense of discussing adolescent problems in class, methods of birth control, sexual diseases?"

"Mummy!" protests Avril.

"Why not?" I reply. "How can you learn, if you don't discuss?"

"But such topics," Mama exclaims. "Are they appropriate? Avril tells me this is what they are doing at her college now."

"It's only done to help us solve our problems," Avril blurts out.

"Problems?" Mama snorts. "Indian children have no problems."

Avril and Ranjan laugh immoderately. Kum-Kum looks disgusted. Rahat, serving tea and biscuits, also laughs. Mama gives him a dirty look. No love lost there. Rahat retreats, but we hear an unnecessary clatter of dishes from his direction as he bombs through the screen door.

"Mummy, you are always so positive about things," says Avril. "We all have problems."

"Ridiculous," says Mama, waving away a biscuit proffered by Ranjan as a quasi-peace offering. "Indian society is much too structured. It is only you, Avril, and you, Ranjan, and not yet you, Kum-Kum, who are rebellious." She turns toward me. "All my children are rebellious, just like me. My oldest daughter broke her Hindu caste to marry a Pakistani Muslim, and now they are living in London. I expect, also, that Avril will marry whom she wants when she wants."

"I expect so," says Avril, smiling at me. She is all dark, sympathetic eyes, with merriment underneath. Her movements are graceful, liquid. All eyes turn toward Avril when she is in the room. What Mama doesn't know is that Avril and I have been meeting four days and nights a week. Avril is tutoring me in Hindi. Mama knows only that Avril is tutoring someone at her college; she doesn't know whom. Avril and I meet in the ice cream store in town, the one place with Ice Station Zebra air-conditioning, so cold you could almost ice skate there. Our courtship is polite, decorous. It has to be, by Indian standards, which are stiffly puritanical. We let Mama run her full course. She thinks she's running the show, so be it. We refer to her as Captain Bligh behind her back.

"Mind you, I don't approve of any of this," Mama states. "Arranged marriages work out very well in India. We do not have this high divorce rate you have in the States. We are not so self-centered. We know that parents make wiser choices for their children."

"Oh, naturally, Mama," Ranjan says, darting a what-can-you-do glance at Avril who stifles a giggle. Mama picks up on this, and by-passes me when she sees I'm ready with an answer and an opinion, to strike a deflecting blow at Kum-Kum. "Kum-Kum, didn't you enjoy those biscuits? You must ask Rahat for the recipe."

Kum-Kum sighs wearily. "How many times, Mummy, have I told you I'm not interested in cooking? I fully intend to marry a man with two servants."

Mama is astonished. We hear an audible intake of air. "Never mind," she snaps out. "Servants get sick. Sometimes knowing how to cook comes in handy."

What really bothers Mama is Kum-Kum's tempo. She is always largo to andante. Mama is inimitably allegro to vivace, all fire and air.

Now it is time to go. Mama thanks Rahat civilly, compliments him on his biscuits, says she will get the recipe another time, shoots out a dagger-eye at Kum-Kum. Mama turns to me. "Did you enjoy that puja?" she asks. Her dazzling smile devours me.

"Very much," I say. "Thanks so much for including me."

"And thank you for the lovely tea," she replies. "We certainly must see more of one another. We have so much to discuss."

Basant Panchmi. The first day of spring. The sky is deep blue now. The fragrance of roses surrounds us from the garden. Mama Bannerjee riding on a peacock. I decide that she is a living Saraswati, loving the old traditions, but proud of her independence and her intellect, sailing full-tilt into whatever uncertainties the future may hold, but stubborn as any goddess has a right to be. Now, she collects Ranjan, Avril, and Kum-Kum, disappears down the verandah past the rose garden, through the poinsettias, out into the yellow dust of Faizabad Road once more.

On the road again, heading home, Mama looks back longingly at the house and says confidentially to Avril, tucked in beside her in the rickshaw. "I do think that Peter Wales would make a splendid match? What do you think?"

"Oh, yes, Mummy," Avril replies. "You always do have such good ideas."

THE SADHU OF FAIZABAD ROAD

A very old man with a white beard and a pink turban, worn Rajasthani style, rather loosely, sits cross-legged under an ancient tamarind tree, just off Faizabad Road. In front of him, he has propped up a shiny, gold metal hand with a finger pointing up to heaven. He fixes me with a knowing look as I dare to pass by. I walk by him every morning at seven o'clock on my way to teach at a women's college in Chand Bagh. He knows all my secrets, I can tell.

Sometimes I see this man tracing futures in the palms of people who have been unable to escape his doomsday glance. They want to know the worst, I suppose. I'd be afraid, I think. I would fear something might be lurking just around the corner. It's probably better not to have any previews of coming attractions.

Faizabad Road amazes me, fascinates me. I don't think it has any end or beginning. Worst of all, it seems to be timeless. It could be five thousand years ago today and I would still be an insubstantial ghost from some odd transmigration joining the thousands of people who move along this street in a strange adagio ballet.

Its music is the screams of birds overhead--the crow and the koel, whose giddy whistle spirals higher in tone through the layers of heat that press down on the road in the afternoon. The counterpoint is provided by the street cries of vegetable and fruit vendors: " *Lal tomater! Gobi, lao, gobi! Kela-wallah, dus annas* ! " Red tomatoes, cauliflowers, and bananas available at only ten annas a dozen!

I have heard weird stories about Faizabad Road. Its history is entangled with that of the Gomati River. Toward one end of town is a settlement called Daliganj, crowded, dirty, with little Hindu temples, a large orthodox Muslim college, and a little Methodist church with a few poverty-stricken parishioners. At the opposite end is Nishatganj, a new marketplace of small, tawdry shops, and vegetable vendors who squat along the road. Beyond Nishatganj, I have heard, the road trails off into open country where snakes and jackals conceal themselves in the jungle thickets flanking the road. The Gomati flows in this direction, also, toward Benares, the sacred city, where it flows into the great mother river, Ganges, which, in turn, pours into the sea. The inhabitants of Chand Bagh tell horrendous tales of jackals stealing away babies by night and of dacoits making murderous attacks on innocent villagers.

Still, the road attracts me. It is pulse, danger, adventure--the mysterious voyage of life. Who could resist it? In the morning mists, it is especially alluring. It feels good, a silky mantle surrounding one, enveloping one, cleansing one, in a way. Against my will, I want to be an anonymous traveler on this mythical pilgrimage to the hidden ends of the earth. I want to join the dark, gypsy-like rickshaw-wallahs, the bearded, red-turbaned sikhs zooming by on bicycles, the Muslim women silently padding along in their white burkas, bare-bottomed babies held tightly in their arms. It is a bizarre motion-picture of a parade, a continuous showing of town merchants machine-gunning along on motor scooters, boys in blue blazers dawdling purposefully on their way to school, scrawny barefooted women with rings in their noses and bangles on their wrists en route to sweep out other people's houses. Mixed in with this high tide of humanity are always water buffaloes and goats being driven along furiously, punctuated every once in a while by a trumpeting elephant or a camel spitting its way through the trudging crowd.

Sometimes, I hear the strangest sounds through the mists. Bagpipe music, for instance, issuing from the Police Reserve Guard Field. I picture platoons of kilted Scotsmen marching, marching, leading the British to victory against the Indians in the nineteenth century, but this is the twentieth century and these are Indian soldiers acting out their Anglo-colonial heritage. I realize the bagpipe itself probably originated in India and was taken to Scotland later, just as the mango from India became the Scottish paisley. Always, India waits to trip up the unwary westerner. Hindi sounds like French, Greeks and Afghanistanis settled in the Chand Bagh area, the Indian people are politer than the English.

I have come here to teach for a year on an exchange program. I bring an American energy and pragmatism to a college that is part of a university system modeled on that of London University in the nineteenth century. I have a master's degree from Harvard, and another master's and a doctorate from Yale. I think I know all the answers. I am punctual, literate, civil, and considerate.

Who is this wise man that materializes under the tree each morning? He must be in his seventies, but he sits, straight-backed, lean, disciplined, like a yoga master. His face is handsome, the features sharp and chiseled, the eyes piercing, the mouth unsmiling. His image challenges me. Would he speak English if I spoke to him?

"Good morning," I say impulsively, giving him a routine smile. I think to myself, that was stupid. I suppose you're going to add "Have a nice day" like a robotic westerner.

"Good morning," the man replies, without looking directly at me. His eyes look down the road. "Your journey will be very short this day."

"I'm just going . . . "

"You're just going to the college where you will teach the English language," he replies.

"You speak English well," I say.

The old man turns his head slowly and looks up at me. "You have a curiosity about Faizabad Road, do you?"

"Not really. I just wondered if you spoke English."

"You must know that the road is love," the old man whispers.

I look at my watch because I realize I've over-stepped my bounds. "I've got to go," I say.

"Yes. I have seen you hurrying by every day. It is the single thread that winds around the world. You may stop to consider." His eyes indicate the gold metal hand.

"Thanks," I say. "Sometime I would like to talk with you further."

He does not reply but looks into the distance again. I almost believe he has extraordinary powers, just as I want to think there is a special magic in India, but I put him out of my mind now. I have fifteen minutes before my first class begins. I walk fast along the road and turn off at the first street which will take me directly to my classroom. Later in the day, when I've finished teaching, I'll deal with Faizabad Road again, but by then the old man will no longer be sitting under the tree.

One morning I'll leave early and wait for his arrival. I'll listen.

WEDDING NIGHT IN JAIPUR

It's nobody's business what I am doing in Jaipur in December. Nobody needs to know who I am. It's enough to know that I broke away from where I was supposed to be and am losing myself in the welcome anonymity that comes from being a runaway in a strange city in a far country. It is not the first time I have done this.

It's cold. Night is creeping up around us. The city is changing. This beautiful city is a gorgeous pink confection melting into the clinging shadows around it. It is full of pirates. Dark, handsome brown faces. White teeth. Gold earrings. Tinsel. Glitter. Orange, yellow, reds, and pinks in their saris and turbans. Shy smiles from women, who suddenly pull their saris protectively around their faces, making me wonder what I have just seen. Lights going on and then off, leaving only the image. Doors closing suddenly, making one guess about what lies behind them.

Chilly night. I button up my wool jacket, turn up the collar against the cold. I am a person of mystery. I am Lord Byron. I am searching for beauty and meaning in the heart of a myth. I am staging a raid on society. One pirate joining all the others. I think I might belong here. I wonder if they'll accept me?

The rickshaw driver insists on a destination. I tell him the bazaar. I say that I want to buy a gold image of Krishna, the god of fine arts. Krishna fluting, Krishna dancing, Krishna in love, Krishna in the hindola, Krishna with the gopis. The driver knows a place.

Fires from little coal pots and oil lamps flicker down low all along the darkening road where we drive. Darkness, dampness now settle over everything. The pirates now become amorphous gypsies huddling over their nourishing fires for warmth. Thick smoke stretches itself indolently around all of us. Sometimes I can see clearly. Othertimes, I dream. Chiaroscuro.

I am aware of a few things. The press of people has grown thicker around me. Up ahead, some bright shafts of rectangular light criss-cross one another over the heads of a moving procession of people. "What is happening?" I ask my driver.

"*Sadhee*," he replies. "You will see the *dhula* instantly."

The *dhula* comes into view high up. This bridegroom is dressed in an elegant silk suit, jeweled turban. He rides on a splendid horse trimmed with silk, brocade, and gold and silver tassels. His friends follow, all carrying over their heads, great crystal chandelier-lanterns, lit by oil. These are what cast up beams of light. There is a clinking, tinkling sound as glass worlds collide.

Darkness again.

Suddenly, another pool of light, another *sadhee*, followed by another area of darkness, and, again, another explosion of light from a new *sadhee*, and the expected mysterious blackness after.

"It is a good night for *sadhees*," says the driver.

The red sandstone Ajmeri Gate looms up in front of us. We are entering the pink city. Thousands of people now form a current that carries us along toward the narrow opening. Suddenly, we are in the middle of another wedding procession. The joyful marchers are chanting. I can see their uplifted faces. The bridegroom, a boy of about sixteen, sits, faintly smiling, high up on a daintily-stepping horse. On another horse nearby rides his younger brother, self-consciously proud, dressed in shining white embroidered silk. The joy, the rhythm sweeps us along faster now.

But just as the bridegroom and his horse are passing me on the right, I feel an odd surge pushing on the left. Another procession is coming toward us with flashing lights overhead, more clinking of chandelier-lanterns. However, the feeling is strangely different. I can hear the low tones of people in sorrow. The instant my rickshaw squeezes next to the flank of the bridegroom's horse, with light from that shining prince in white silk spilling down brightly on me, the central object in the other procession passes by on the left, so close that I can almost touch it. I hold my breath. High above the shoulders of the mourners, on wooden boards, and wrapped in white linen, goes a corpse being borne in quick-step toward a burning ghat for cremation. So thinly wrapped is it that I can see the crepe-like body beneath it with the hands gently folded across the stomach.

One instant of life and death so close together on a single vibrating string with me in the middle, the idol seeker, the searcher for meanings. Just one second only did I feel the pulse of it. Then it changed. A confusing flash of lights, a powerful thrust forward, and, in a rush, we are propelled by some invisible force through the narrow Ajmeri Gate into the larger world of the pink city's bazaar itself.

"Please pull over," I shout to the driver. I am almost breathless from this frightening encounter which seemed like an unexpected, unwanted ritual birth. We stop, but we are in front of a small Hindu shrine where a crowd of people are clapping their hands and chanting, "*Ram, ram, hare, hare*" while offering flowers, money, and other gifts to the illuminated idol inside. The smoky air is rose-colored and heavy now. I cannot breathe.

The driver directs me to a shop. "Will you have this Krishna for decorative purposes, or do you wish it to worship?" the kindly shopkeeper smiles at me.

I do not know what to say to him. I turn to my driver. Does he see the terror in my eyes? But he only returns the same kind of understanding smile as the shopkeeper.

VIAJES AUTOBUS AZUL

Hello. We are now having the welcome drink in Madrid, as says it on your schedule. I am Omar, to be your tour guide on Viajes Autobus Azul through Spain, Gibraltar, Morocco, and Portugal. I am student in Tangier where I am perfecting the English at American Linguistic Institute and earning the money for studies by leading the tours. I am chosen for this by Viajes Autobus Azul in Madrid because I am speaking the English, French, Arabic, Spanish and Portuguese languages. My hometown is Ceuta which is what is left of Spanish Morocco in Africa. Is very beautiful port on coast. We will be crossing there from Algeciras.

I am Muslim in religion and will be telling you many things when we are arriving in Morocco. You would like to know there are four Americans, seven English peoples, two from New Zealand, four Australians, two from India, one lady from British Columbia, one man from South Africa and four from Indonesia in this group. You have all received our blue blazer and our blue travel bag that says "Viajes Autobus Azul" on it, have you not?

And this is Reynaldo who is from Madrid. He is to be our driver on this bus which we are taking with us on the tour. Now, here is our sangria. You have liked this, yes? It is the national drink of Spain. If you are a good Muslim, you are not supposed to drink, but if you are not so good, you can have something sometimes, if you wish. So I have something, I think.

Here's cheers to a good voyage.

MADRID: This is the capital of all Spain, but it is not a city. It is a town. King Philip II has declared it to be the capital, but has forgotten to name it a city, so it is still a town, a villa.

TOLEDO: You may have noticed that the synagogue is called St. Mary's. You may have wondered why. It is very curious, is it not, that it is built in architectural style of the Moors, which is Muslim. I will tell you why. It is that first the Moors are here and they have built this in their style. And it is in a poor section so the Jews can purchase it for a synagogue, but they cannot afford to fix it up to make the changes, so it stays the same. Then when the Catholic church says everybody must become Christians or leave, it still stays the same.

Visigoths founded Toledo. In 711 the Moors have conquered the city. And then in 1085 comes King Alfonso VI with some Christianity. It remained as a synagogue until 14th century when Saint Vicente Ferrer has made a violent protest against the Jews and it has become a Catholic church, Santa Maria la Blanca.

That lady who is carrying with her the photography. It is defended to take the photographs with the flash. It could set off the alarms by fault.

SEVILLE: This is the cathedral of Seville. You are standing in front of the tomb of Christopher Columbus. It was put here in 1902 just in time for the exposition of Seville. If you are in Santo Domingo, they say also that Christopher Columbus is buried there. Perhaps it is true. He could be buried in both places. It is known that he died in Valladolid in 1506. Then somehow his body came to Cuba in 1796, next, to Haiti, and back again to Spain in 1899. They have done some x-rays and they shows that some bones in Seville are from the time he died and some are recent, and the x-rays have revealed the same is true of Santo Domingo. So who knows?

Perhaps is some parts of Columbus here and some in El Salvador.

Ah, here is the American lady who is famous for the shopping. What you have bought today? Did you buy that silver chalice in the cathedral? I have seen you were talking with one priest about it.

Now look at this. It is Plaza de Espana. It is not old, but was built in a hurry for the exposition to represent all Spain, and you will see all of Spain's counties represented in tiles here. You have already seen this many times. Did you see *Lawrence of Arabia?* Do you remember Peter O'Toole comes down these steps? Then when you see the Alcazar, you will see where it has also been used in *Reds* with Warren Beatty. You will observe also that our statue of El Cid that you will see in the city looks very much like Charlton Heston.

Seville is the town of Carmen, Lord Byron's Don Juan, and the famous barber. This is the cigarette factory that maybe Carmen worked in. It is now the university.

The gypsies have traditionally lived across the Guadalquivir river in the section called Triana. Hold on to your pocketbooks and do not show your jewelry in the public places. They will, how you say, snatch it off your arm.

Alfonso, who has taken our group photograph today in front of the cathedral, is a gypsy from Triana. Gypsies are very good photographers. Some peoples say they have the evil eye that can see into your soul. So you must be very careful and not to look too closely at any of them, even Alfonso. They can tell all your secrets. I don't want him to catch my eyes, so I don't look at him never.

VILA BOIM, PORTUGAL: This is a Roman aquaduct. It is very tall, built with arches and bricks. It looks modern, does it not? You see, the Romans were everywhere in the empire. On the other side is an hotel. We will stop here for one hour for the lunch.

Well, how you like the lunch? It is one simple village cafe, but you have chance to see how it is in the countryside.

How did you like the restrooms? You did select some trees?

Some of you have noticed we are now missing the gentleman from Indonesia and the three women with him. I have called him Henry and his wives because he is rich Muslim and I cannot figure out who is wife and who is not. He can have four wives, if he wish. I am thinking he already has three. They did not come with us into Portugal because is forgotten to obtain visa. Henry has said to the customs that he has been told to get visa at border. But customs has said to him, "How can you get visa when is not diplomatic relations between Indonesia and Portugal?" Henry and his wives will wait in Spain and join us later in Algeciras, when we make the return. I have put them into taxicab and sent them ahead. Is expensive, but I have called Madrid and they will be paying. So, lesson is, don't go into country if your country don't have diplomacy.

We are now missing one person. Where is it? Oh, there it is. It is now sitting in the seat. Good. Now we can go.

LISBON: This coach you are standing before has belonged to King John. He has made it for to impress the Pope in Vatican with the power of Portugal because he has not believed that Portugal is powerful enough. The Pope has not liked King John because King John has had two sons by a nun and the Pope is not pleased. So King John has to find a way to convince the Pope and he has caused to be built these coaches to make a procession in front of the Pope.

If you want to undrink your morning coffee and orange juice, we will be making here a brief stop for rest.

ON THE COAST OF PORTUGAL: Today we are so happy to have Reynaldo back with us after our bus did break down on the way to Sintra which we could not see. It was the fuel pump. The bus cannot go when the fuel pump refuses to work, but Reynaldo has had it fixed, and we did have a substitute bus with cowboy driver which was exhilarating, was it not?

CALDAS DA RAINHA: You see there it is the market. The women. They are coming every morning just to buy a little bit, what they need for the day. They like everything fresh. And for the soliciting. To talk. To have coffee. To discuss the things of the day.

OBIDOS: They have built the city walls all around on the top of the hill to control, to look if anybody is approaching, so they can defend. It is a twelfth-century idea.

NAZARE: This is a charming fishing village where, of course, the fishermen are doing their fishing.They go every day in their bare feet. See how white the sand is. Many peoples come here for the pleasure. You can just rent a room from the residents or you can have a tent on the beach. You can see the cable car just appearing on the cliff. It is the way to go to the top where you can have the most picturesque view.

NEAR COIMBRA: This is the shrine of Fatima. In 1916 three young children looking up at the sky saw apparition of Virgin Mary in oak tree. It is time of first world war. Europe had already been at war for three years. They was named Lucia, Francisco, and Jacinta. The Virgin told them to come back to the oak tree on the thirteenth of each month for five months. On July 13th, she said a miracle would appear in October. Then the children were taken away and the Virgin again appeared and did say to speak the rosary every day and to take communion. If they don't do this, then Russia will make the trouble for all the world. And many others did see this appearance of the Virgin.

Two of the children died in 1919 and 1920, but Lucia became a nun and lived in Coimbra which is near where we will be spending the night. And there is a fountain that did spring up after the children did see this sight, and there is also the oak still there that you can see. And Lucia is still alive.

She is eighty-five years old. She live somewhere in Coimbra, in a nunnery, I think.

CURIA: This is our hotel tonight. You remember our hotel in Lisbon, all glass and marble? Forget about it. This is now totally different. For a contrast, we have the beautiful Palace Hotel da Curia with its magnificent gardens, swimming pool, and tennis courts. We will have one good night's sleep here. You do like it, yes?

BEJA: You must have noticed the difference between Spain and Portugal. We say they are behind most of the countries of central Europe in progress because of lack of highways and because of physical separation by Pyrennees Mountains. There is a great difference between country like Portugal and, say, France, although both have some similarity, like Fatima is to Portugal what Lourdes is to France. I mean, the Virgin made an appearance also, and so forth.

But even between Spain and Portugal there is a difference. Although both now have joined the European economical community, it will take a few years. You can see now the progress coming into Spain, but Portugal is still behind. It was partly also the political situation with Franco as dictator in Spain. All that has isolated these two countries from rest of Europe. But I'm sure that in a few years there will be some better roads and more progress.

We are going today I wish I knew. No, just kidding. Do you see that sign? It says to pay attention, to keep your mind watchful on the road, you know.

Where is Mrs. Heyman? Has she got lost again? I am going to have to put a leash on her.

ALGECIRAS: Do you see that boat just leaving the port? That is our boat leaving for Africa. We have missed it. When I ask for the tickets, they say they know nothing about it. I have had to call Madrid to ask them what is what. We will find a place now to have the lunch and then we will catch the next boat. We shall be very late arriving in Casablanca tonight.

But, look, we have welcomed back Henry and his wives who have had fantastic adventure in taxi and have been swimming in the sea for past three days on Costa del Sol. Hello, Henry. Hello, women. Welcome back to our group.

TANGIER, MOROCCO: We are now entering the American section of Tangier. There are many big homes of rich peoples here like Malcolm Forbes who has given us this museum of military battles. Rich Americans and Europeans have liked to live here because is very restful and much beautiful. Barbara Hutton, a millionairess, lives here. We like to say in Tangier she is so rich she can buy any husband she like. She has two houses here. One in this sector and another in the Casbah. Is very nice lady. I see her sometimes in town. Is older now, but is very pleasant and generous to everybody.

What you are saying, mister? You are Fred of Australia, are you not? Yes, I thought so. No, it cannot be possible that Barbara Hutton and Malcolm Forbes are dead. If they were dead, then why would I see them? Would I lie to you? No, your newspapers are wrong. They walk around. I see them sometimes. Don't believe everything you read. Just believe me.

MOROCCO: We are just coming into the Rif Mountains. You can see all around us acres of sunflowers. Look there. You see Moroccan shepherds putting up hay on donkeys. See, their carts are laden with branches. Looks like a walking tree blocking the road. Reynaldo will have to blow the bus horn at them. It will do no good. Watch, they do not move.We will just go very slow past them. Look, the shadows from clouds that roll over the pastures. How beautiful it is, yes? Here is little village coming up. See, in those sidewalk cafes you see only men and boys squatting in front looking at us curiously. More tourists, they say. They are waving now. These villagers inhabit low huts with white-washed walls. Prickly pears make a kind of fence for their properties.

Some Berbers live at Larache, left over from Spanish Civil War. Generalissimo Franco began his campaign here, fighting against Moroccans. That purple flower, very brilliant, is bougainvillea. It makes many hedges here. Look, that garden, you see rose bushes in full bloom.

TETOUAN: We are just coming into Tetouan where the main industry is the black market. The people are just crossing into Ceuta where they make purchases of video cameras and other products and bring them back into Tetouan where is a big business in black market and much profit. Then the second big industry is agriculture. Marijuana is the biggest crop. Is exported to all over the world. Then the next is phosphates. Then the fourth is tourism like all of us, you'll see.

This arena you are looking at was built for two hundred and two persons, so you can see it is very big. There is also room for standing people.

CASABLANCA: This is the third largest city in Africa. Is a city of about twenty-five million. Is a very romantic city. You are remembering it from the movie called *Casablanca*. It is called that because someone has built a white house and after that everyone is wanted to have a white house--and so is called Casablanca. It is the largest city of Morocco, but is not the capital. Rabat is the capital. It is there that Mohammed V has his tomb. It is very beautiful. To the south is the Sahara of Morocco. The Sahara has been in dispute with Algeria for a long time, but is all right now. We have been having good relations with Algeria for two weeks.

RABAT: You do see those white birds sitting in the trees all along the road? You are looking at tonight's dessert. Pigeon pie is a specialty in Morocco. We will be going this evening to a real Moroccan palace in the medina where you will be eating these birds for dinner. And we will be taking you to buy carpets, if you wish, and to drink mint tea. You cannot go alone. You must go with me and a special guide, because you could be getting lost. Everybody will please keep their eyes on Mrs. Heyman.

FEZ: You will be seeing the oldest university in the world in the world's largest medina. The students are studying the Koran there, law, and philosophy, and the medina is just the same as it was in the eighth century because the streets is so small they cannot change. Only the donkeys and people can go in these streets. There is also the section for Jews called the mellah. In all Arab cities, the section called mellah is for the Jews. There is not much Christians in this city. Here is now just coming a cemetery where is buried many Muslims with the tombs facing mostly toward the east which is toward Mecca. You may have noticed our sunflowers in the field is not facing toward the sun like other flowers, but do face the east also, toward Mecca.

Now, you must listen to me when I tell you something important, for your safety. That American lady who was just going to look with the man at carpets upstairs. I am to tell you it is not carpets he has. It is sex. I have heard him say in French to invite you to have sex with him and you have said yes. I know you did not know what you said. But there is not carpets, only sex. You know what is sex? You have this thing in California?

CEUTA: This is my hometown. This is my house, my mother, my five brothers and two sisters. We all live here in great happiness. See, how my mother is smiling. She is very shy person. Muslim women do not like to show their face outside the family. For you, she make big exception. She is so proud her son hangs around with Americans and English. Hello, Mama, how it goes today? This is my tour group. She say, she will pose for photographs with all tourists. That is my brother Karim. There, Arshad, Mahmood, Qamar, little one Husaini. Sisters are Sabhia and Rizwana. Rizwana is to study to be a doctor. Is very advanced. Our father runs video store in town. Is too busy to be here. Makes much money. Yes, you can give my mother some tips. She is enjoying to have souvenirs from tourists. She say she has large family. Loves dollars and pounds. Arshad works in black market. He can get good rates for her.

Thank you, Mama. Thank you, brothers and sisters. Now we go through mountains to collect our boat across the Mediterranean. We are to stay in Costa del Sol in Torremolinos. Is very fashionable resort. Many English stay in Marbella nearby. There you will get good cup of tea, Mr. and Mrs. Jessup. I know you do not like our mint tea.

How you like my country? Is very beautiful, yes? Full of many excitements. Good food. People are friendly. They say, come visit, we love tourists.

Next time you come, you go south to Sahara. Is very different in desert. You can ride on camels. Is very hot. I do not like it much. I prefer Madrid. I like many nightclubs, many dancing girls. But, of course, I am young student. What you expect? I love to explain tours to peoples on bus. Viajes Autobus Azul is very good thing, I think, for me and for you. Is an education, is it not?

Now, as we descend the mountains to our ship again, I will play you some music of Morocco. You will notice the fields again, the flowers, see the peoples who will wave to you. Now you are just beginning to notice the Mediterranean Sea again. It is just out there that it meets with the Atlantic. Can you see the two colors--the green one and the blue, two oceans who are coming together?

Look, Fred and Peg from Australia and Harry from South Africa have fallen asleep. They have missed everything today, I'm afraid.

You know, sometimes when I see tourists misbehave like this, I think to leave them in the countryside where they can live with the Berbers to see how they like it. They should pay attention when they have paid good money to go with Viajes Autobus Azul and not drink so much the beer as I did see Fred and Harry do last evening. Many English love the beer too much, I think.

Well, let them sleep away. The rest will keep all eyes and ears open in case you only arrive in Morocco once. Soon we will be coming to our ship again and then it will be goodbye, Africa, hello, Europe.

I will be turning off the microphone now, so this is all you will be hearing from me. Enjoy the music, please. And the vision.

CASTLEMARTYR

One image dominates: A woman sits on a brown mohair couch with a shawl drawn around her shoulders. She seems old, tired. Her body is stooped, defeated somehow. She has straight hair, a tired face, but light blue, intelligent eyes. She is combing her thin, greyish hair. I want to help. She lets me. I climb up and stand on the couch behind her. I comb her hair. It is too fine and frayed. I try to comb it as well as I can. I want to make it beautiful. I cannot. She smiles at me. She is gentle with me. My mother pulls me away from her. She reaches out her fingers to mine. We touch in parting, fingertips to fingertips, as though one of us is drowning.

This is my grandparents' house. It seems large and mysterious to me, often ominous. I am afraid of burglars. I am afraid of kidnappers. I am afraid of murderers. This house has been robbed five times. The last time, in the dead of winter, the burglar climbed in through the high window in the pantry. He left huge footprints in the snow. The police were amazed. He must have been some giant of a man.

Once, when burglars broke into the back of the house, my grandmother and my aunt, who were home at the time, had to climb out on the roof from my grandparents' bedroom in the front of the house. This roof covers the long wrap-around porch below. My grandmother and aunt had to sit on the roof in their nightgowns after midnight calling for help from the neighbors. All of this scares me. There is a third floor here, where I usually have to sleep, and a dark attic chock full of stuff right across from my room. There is a maze-like basement that wanders underneath the entire house and has a separate entrance to the outside. I am convinced there are four or five burglars and murderers who live in dark caves down there.

There are stained-glass Tiffany windows, a long polished banister, good for sliding down, a window seat on the lower landing, parlor doors that open and close like a theatre, a very narrow secret passage of stairs that go up from the kitchen into the servants' quarters, and a detached garage way out in the back; another hideout for thugs and killers, I am sure.

The garden has an apple tree with very few apples on it, but the ones that are there are delicious. I know that for a fact. I plucked an apple from the tree one day and ate it. I didn't realize my grandfather counted the apples. He does. He is Scottish and very fierce. His voice is loud. I was actually trembling when he boomed out, "Who took an apple from my tree?" I was afraid he might sentence me to permanent hell in the basement along with the other thieves, but he didn't. My grandmother appeared, put her arm around me, and said to my grandfather, "Hush now. You've no business raising your voice like that." She is Irish. That accounts for all her good qualities, says my mother.

Their living room, dining room, and front parlor all have beautiful Chinese rugs in them. The one in the parlor is blue. There are dragons and peacocks in the design of the rug. The one in the living room is red. A great nightingale hangs from a tree in this one. The rug in the dining room is green. Birds fly around in a golden Chinese heaven in this one. My sister, brother, and I love to lie on the floor and play on these rugs. We each have a collection of marbles. We carry them around in boxes--you know, like Lord and Taylor's or Bloomingdale's boxes left over from Christmas. Our marbles have names. They are pupils in the imaginary school we run. We are the teachers. We have an intercom system that runs to all three of our bedrooms at home. "Miss Curtis," I will call to Jenny on the phone. "How is John F. Kennedy doing in school?"

"Not as well as he should," she will reply. "He needs to do more work in Math. He only managed a C+ on the last exam."

"Thank you," I say. "I will speak to him about it. Has Sophia Loren gotten off probation yet?"

"Yes," Jenny says. "In fact, she just got an A in Geography."

"Good," I reply. Our marbles are not just ordinary students. Many of them are very well known people. Did you know that Julius Caesar and Joan of Arc both went to our school? Joan was valedictorian when she graduated.

What we do with our pupils is we take them on field trips to China. We think these glassies, purees, and aggies look beautiful against the patterns of the Chinese rugs, and so we roll them around and play games with them all day. The adults have to step over us delicately when all three of us are in the same room at the same time. Of course we have to be extra careful when my grandfather comes into the room. We don't want him to raise that loud Scottish voice. My grandmother, on the other hand, when she was able to, used to get down on our level and play with us. "Oh, that's a good looking pupil," she would say, watching us spin a marble.

"She should be," says Jenny. "She's a champion figure skater. She's Sonja Henie."

When we're not playing games with our marbles, we are reading from the great stacks of *National Geographic* magazines my grandfather has. He lets us take old copies he doesn't want anymore and we use them in our school back home. Jenny is the librarian. She catalogues everything. We have a shelf in our family's library where we keep all our school stuff. Harpo is the kindergarten teacher. He has to be. He's so young that he doesn't really have any subjects yet he can teach--just general material. We don't let him give any grades either. Jenny knows French and Math. She also teaches Latin and Spanish, although she really hasn't started studying Spanish. I teach sports and English and coach all the teams. I turn out winning teams. My homeroom plays Harpo's and Jenny's homerooms and my marbles always win.

In the summer my grandparents go to the shore and take all of us with them. Their place is on an island. You have to take a boat to get there, and once you are there, there are very few cars. We walk everywhere and take wagons with us to carry things. My mother loves it at the shore and so does my grandmother. She says it reminds her of home--Ireland--although it is very different. But she likes the sound of the ocean roaring up and drawing back from the beach at night. She says it makes her sleep better.

My grandfather continues working through the summer. He seems never to stop. He comes to visit us on weekends and arrives on the boat from the mainland. We all go down to meet him. My mother says we have all run out of money by that time and need more if we're to get through next week. My grandmother always says, "Whisht now, let me handle this."

When the boat lands, we scan the faces to see what kind of mood my grandfather might be in. If there is a dark cloud on his face, we know business didn't go so well that week and he might be in a very grumpy mood. But my grandmother rushes to meet him first, kisses him, and says, "Welcome, darlin', the island is yours. They've been asking for you all week long. 'When is he coming?' they say. 'Will he be here again this Friday?'" That usually gets him. I can see his face light up. Then he might take out a $100 bill and say to me,"Run to the store and get me some cigars." If he does, we know we're home free. We all breathe a sigh of relief. Once he didn't even ask me to give back the change.

I don't think my grandfather really loves the island as much as the rest of us do, though. My mother says he really is a city man because he came from a small town in Scotland and made good in America. But anything my grandmother wants is all right with him. I call her "Nana" and him "Dada." She is so much fun. I love to hear her talk. Her voice goes up and down the scale with a kind of music in it. She is really very nice and very funny.

Once, my mother went out swimming in the ocean and nearly drowned. She waved her hand in the air for help, and, Nana, sitting on the beach, thought she was waving hello and waved right back. I was frightened when my mother told me this story, but everyone laughed and thought it was very funny, so I guess it was all right.

My mother said that when Harpo was born on George Washington's birthday, my father came home from the hospital and said to Nana, "Hip, hip, hooray! George Washington has been born!" Nana simply said, "Whisht now, get up to bed like a good fellow and nobody will know anything about it." She whisked him up the stairs and into bed, thinking he was drunk. He wasn't. He was just happy that Harpo was here at last.

Jenny looks like Nana. That's what my mother says and anybody else you ask. I look like Dada, unfortunately. That means I have red hair and freckles and a permanently sour puss. My mother says that's the way all Scotsmen look. The Irish are beautiful, she says. She is lucky. She and Jenny and Nana are all beautiful. I look like the ugly Scottish side of the family, obviously. And Harpo? We don't know who he takes after. He has a crooked little smile and a mop of blond hair. He's just a Harpo. That's what he is, a little clown of a brother.

When the weekend is over, Dada goes back to the city. We all go to the boat to wave goodbye to him. After he leaves we have one big party all week long. Nana plays games with us and walks along the beach where we all pick up beach glass. "All green glass comes from Ireland," says Nana. We love to sing "When Irish Eyes are Smiling" full out to the wind slapping in our faces.

"Tell me about Ireland," I say. "What is it like? When can I go?"

"It's directly across the ocean," Nana says, looking out to sea. "It's a small country and a poor one, but it's a poetic country."

"Tell me about the horses, Nana," says Jenny.

"Is it as nice as this island?" asks Harpo.

"I want to go to a poetic country, Nana," I plead.

"Well, you will someday, my darlin'," says Nana, swooping down and kissing me in a rush. I like it when she does that. I think everything about her is grand.

One of her best stories is about how she went back to Ireland with Dada. She leans close to us when she tells it. "Oh, we went in style,"she tells us. "Nothing but the best. Deluxe all the way. Himself would have a great pompous limousine and a chauffeur to drive it, no less. Can you imagine the look on the faces of all my friends when we showed up in that contraption? I told him he was overdoing it a bit, but you know your grandfather. You can't tell him much."

In his business, Dada had offices in Paris and New York. Nana said he would never fly, but only go on ships. "We tried them all," she said. "All the Queens, the Brittanic, Liberté, Ile de France, United States, but now we're running out of ships. There are fewer crossings every year. I don't know what Himself will do after I'm gone."

When the summer was over, Jenny got Nana to come to her Geography class to talk about Ireland. Harpo's class and mine were invited to attend. It was rare that Nana and Dada came to our house at all. We lived too far away from the city, Dada said, and he thought that there was everything anyone ever needed in the city. Why would anyone live in the suburbs, he asked?

Anyway, they came just for the day. We had the usual roast lamb, which my grandfather required, with the boring mint jelly and the shortbread after dinner, and all. And then school was in session upstairs and Nana went up the wooden hill with us to Jenny's room where she spoke to the marbles about Ireland.

"Mrs. MacVuirach," Jenny began, glancing down at her list of prepared questions. "When did you first come to America?"

"When I was seventeen," Nana said with a wink at Harpo and me. We started to giggle, but Jenny stopped us.

"What was the reason for your emigration?" Jenny said. Jenny is sometimes so snotty about using big words that Harpo doesn't know and that I'm not really sure of.

"Well, to become a nurse in the United States," said Nana.

"Aren't there nurses in Ireland?" Jenny said.

"Well, yis. That's where I got me early training. But the finest hospitals were in New York. I knew that. And I came here to live with me cousins."

"What was the reaction in your family when you left Ireland?"

"Well, now, dearie, a lot of me brothers were gettin' the hell out too, ye know."

"Uncle Jack?" said Harpo.

"Yis," said Nana. "Jack went to Canada, Dick went to London, and me sister Agnes went to New Zealand. There wasn't anybody left at home."

"Where was home, Nana?" I asked." Tell us about the rich lord."

"Home was quite simple. County Cork. A wee town called Castlemartyr. And the rich lord, he was sent from England. He had a big castle at the other end of town. We were all scared to death of him."

"Is it green?" asked Harpo. "Is Ireland green the way it is on the globe?"

"It's green all right," said Nana. "The winds and mists chase 'round the island and make it green and beautiful."

Her eyes looked tired, but they lit up when she told us about a play by an Irish poet. It was the tale of an old woman, very worn and ancient, who became a beautiful young woman again by some magic. I loved the way she told it, like a song, her voice rising and falling with the music of it.

An idea struck me. "Nana, tell me the truth. Wasn't that play written about you?"

"No, no, darlin'," she said. "Not about me. About *all* Ireland."

My mother looked in and said, "Is school over yet, children? I think Dada wants to get back to town."

"Oh, we mustn't keep him waiting," said Nana, getting up. "We've got to get Himself back to his beloved town." I noticed that she seemed a little dizzy when she walked. I saw my mother's eyes dart quickly to hers. I wondered what that meant.

I saw Nana only once more after that. She was propped up in an ocean of pillows in her huge mahogany bed and could barely smile and wave at Jenny, Harpo, and me. We brought flowers to her. I presented them to her. Her fingers seemed to want to touch mine rather than hold the flowers. The nurse said we could stay only ten minutes. Harpo spoiled it and began to cry, and so the nurse pushed us out of the room. We only had that one last minute with her.

That's the final thing I remember about my grandmother--just her nice smile, her kind blue eyes, and her fingertips slipping away from mine.

Then back home again my mother would some-times talk on the phone and afterwards have tears in her eyes. "They are closing me out," she said to me one day. "They won't let us in to see her anymore."

Jenny talked to Mother and told Harpo and me that she learned Nana was dying from cancer. We had our pupils send cards, one in the shape of a shamrock, but it didn't do any good. Nana died and that was that. We had to stay at home with an aunt and an uncle while my mother and father went to the funeral. They were gone for days. My mother told us later that it really was an Irish wake with everyone laughing and drinking, one big party. She said she thought the neighbors were scandalized. "But that's the way she would have wanted it," said my mother.

And the sad thing is that within a year Dada was gone also. "Dead of a broken heart," said my mother. "He just couldn't survive without her," my father said to my mother. Jenny took me aside and told me, but not Harpo because she didn't think he would understand, that Nana and Dada were actually like Romeo and Juliet, star-crossed lovers.

That left us now without any grandparents. The last trace was when they broke up my grandparents' house. Their three children all took different things. The Chinese rugs went three different ways. One uncle took the green rug. My aunt took the red rug. And my mother took the blue rug. I remember that sad day after the house was finally sold and I stood with my mother on the porch as she turned the key in the lock of the front door. "Goodbye," she said. "Goodbye, Nana. Goodbye, Dada," I said. My mother had tears in her eyes, but I was secretly happy I wouldn't have to stay overnight in that burglar haven ever again.

Among the things my mother found when she went over all the papers my grandparents had left behind: a card in the shape of a shamrock colored with green crayon reading "Miss Curtis' Fourth Grade wishes you 'Top of the Morning'," a flock of poems written by my grandmother when she was sixteen in Ireland, a handwritten note from Nana to my mother requesting that some of her money be used "for the children's education and to send them on a happy journey to Ireland one day," and a note written in my shakiest, most scared handwriting, reading,

"Dear Dada,
I am sorry I stole
one apple.
Like,
Your Grandson."

I think I was telling him something by signing it "Like" instead of "Love."

The bus rumbles into town. What a rough journey we had coming up from Cork. The bus driver couldn't resist stopping at every other pub along the way for a bucket of suds, and so we clanked our way along slowly and irregularly, stopping here and there, letting people on and off wherever they wished, and letting the bus driver run into whatever pub he wanted to.

Castlemartyr at last! I see a church on a hill in the center of town. There are tombstones sticking up all around it. You can't get to the church itself without waltzing through this Irish bone orchard. Up I go to the door, look in, flush out an old woman with a broom, probably napping when she's supposed to be sweeping.

"Well, what is it? What d'ye want?" Hostile, angry at being found out.

"My grandmother came from this town. I thought I might find some family tombstones."

"Well, if she's Catholic, they have their church at the other end of town."

"No. As a matter of fact, she was Church of Ireland."

"Church of Ireland? That's what this is. What was her name?"

"Mary Flood."

"Mary Flood?"

"Yes. I'm her grandson."

"Mary Flood's grandson? God love ye, her father was the stone mason in town. Those are all the Flood graves there. You'll notice they've the finest tombstones in the yard. Henry Flood carved them all."

A tour of the cemetery. The Welcome Wagon is on. The caretaker is hospitable now, all Irish charm and stories, wanting news of my grandmother, dead these many years. There wasn't much to tell. She died of cancer in her fifties, my grandfather one year later of grief, they said. She was, I think, the bright spot in all our lives, the leavening, the creative spark, the touch of humor.

"There's Will Ahearn," the lady said. "And Sallie Ferguson. They were friends of your grandmother's. Come. We'll ring them up. Where's your car and chauffeur?"

"There aren't any," I said. "I came here on the local bus."

"On the bus? Did ye, now?" Incredulity that the grandson of Mary Flood should travel on a bus. I could see my grandfather's hand in all this.

"The last time your grandmother and grandfather was here, they arrived in fine style with a limousine and driver."

"I know," I said. "But I'm just a poor graduate student."

"G'wan," she said. "All Americans is rich."

"Not this one," I said, realizing even as I said it that all things are relative.

"Well, we'll walk then. Sallie and Will will be thrilled to see youse."

They were. They beamed affection. Sallie, tall, garrulous, an animated hawk--"Your grandmother lived here. The roof was thatch, the ground floor was dirt until she was ten years old. She studied nursing in Dublin, then went on the boat to New York, worked at St. James' Hospital where she met your grandfather who was a patient there. They only came back here twice, you know. God love ye, could you lend us a fiver? Me daughter's working in the crutch factory."

And Will Ahearn, probably in his late seventies or early eighties, a tall, rangy, giggling, blue-eyed man with no teeth, but a wonderfully appreciative smile. He leaned close to me: "God love youse. I never married for love of Mary Flood. What did she croak of?"

I felt like lying and saying, "She pined away from love of such a darlin' man as you, Will," but instead I told him the truth. His face clouded over. "That was a dirty shame, that was," is all he said.

"Can you stay the night?" Sallie Ferguson asked.

"No."

"Will ye come to dinner?"

"Can't. Have to catch the six o'clock bus, heading north to Sligo and County Mayo."

"Will ye come to tea?"

"I will come to tea if you'll let me treat."

To the local inn, then, where the tea party grew to twenty-five good souls as the news spread. "Come over here, Robert O'Flahertie. He's come all the way from America. Mary Flood's grandson he is."

"Is he, indeed?"

The conviviality welled up. Always an occasion when an American comes home, always an opportunity for more stories of success and prosperity in the New World.

And then the farewells, the embraces, the promises to write and keep in touch, with the bus arriving, the hands slipping away, the fingertips barely touching, and the bus pulling out, clanking on to a new destination in a world illuminated by lightning.

THE GOODBYES

Niall saw the distant patch of a promising Welsh day dawning outside his small bedroom window high up. He grasped the hard wood of his bed with both hands, sorry now that the day he dreaded had come at last. For six months he had wondered what it would finally be like. Would he be retching with nervousness, exhilarated by his own decisiveness, or banking down tears when he left the old mother and father? What he didn't know is that his last day at home would be a poem that he would never forget.

He got up cautiously from his bed, pulled on his clothes over his long white body. He heard a scuttling noise downstairs and knew that his mother was up and about like him, earlier than usual. He went down to the kitchen, noticed that she carefully hid her concern from him while serving him his cornflakes in too fussy a manner. "You'll say something to your Dad? He'll be coming down soon."

"Yes."

The father appeared, maroon cardigan buttoned tight, said not a word, nor did Neill. The father ate no breakfast, communicating only with his eyes to his wife, who understood the powerful sound of his silence.

"Dad," said Niall. "I wanted to say . . . "

The father pressed Niall hard on the shoulder so that the boy smelled the sweetish accumulated smoke from many pipes of tobacco. Niall looked at his father expectantly, but in the same glance he wondered why his father had diminished so much in his estimation. He decided it was education that made the difference. The father caught the boy's appraising glance, turned, and went away to work in the factory at Dowlais, as he had done for almost the entire twenty-five years of his son's life. A certain heaviness went out of the room with him. Both mother and son felt it.

Niall gathered up his worn university bookpack and his duffel, kissed his mother, smiled at her, hugged her chicken shoulders in a way that embarrassed him because she seemed so breakable suddenly, and stepped out into the welcome sunlight of relief.

He decided to walk. He came first to the church of St. Tydfil where he saw some workmen buzzing around a scaffold they were putting up over the side entrance. "How are you, Evan?" he called out to his friend. "What are you doing today?"

"Taking the church apart and putting it back together," said the pirate, Evan, throwing a rope in Niall's direction.

"Not me," said Niall. "Not today."

He came next to Howland & Sons, Ltd., looked in and saw Dame Gladys shoveling up some tin loaves next to the Bloomer and Swansea loaves. "What are you doing, Dame Gladys?" he asked.

"I'm putting up loaves to make sandwiches and toasties for the likes of you, luv," she said.

"Not today," he said, laughing, giving her a smart military salute, hand against forehead.

The sun felt good on him. The world became a soft sculptured golden bowl as he walked along. The Glamorgan hills seemed covered with bright green velvet. The sunshine brought out a great many people and spread a special pleasantness in town that day.

He saw Tom Davies at the entrance to W. H. Smith's. "Hail, choirmaster," he called out.

"Hail, Niall Cynfyn," replied Tom Davies.

He stopped at the newsagent, bought a copy of *The Guardian* to read on the train. "Twenty-five pence," said the newsagent, holding out his hand.

"Thank you," said Niall, adding, "What a nice day."

"Lovely," said the newsagent, shielding himself from the sun with a newspaper to see who it was that was so courteous today.

Niall kept on walking until he ran into Old Baillie at the turning to the station.

"Good morning, Niall," croaked Old Baillie. "Back to Oxford, are you?"

"Not today," said Niall.

"Well, don't forget us here. There's a lot of knowledge in our library."

"I know that," replied Niall. He turned the corner, walked into the railway station and said to Dave Carter, the ticket agent. "One way to Cardiff, please, Dave."

"Cardiff?" questioned Dave, handing him the ticket. "Here it is."

"And to London from Cardiff," added Niall.

"London, is it?" asked Dave, writing out the ticket.

"Yes, thank you," said Niall, taking the ticket and adjusting the duffel dangling from his shoulder.

He walked down the platform, sat on a bench, looked at the handsome wall mural of the town's history presented as a gift from the school children of Merthyr Tydfil. A skinny young punk with black leather pants and a white tank top that read, "Please don't remove this t-shirt, it's holding up my tits," sat next to him. He recognized him as Mrs. Murray's son. "Hello, Ian," he said. "What are you doing today?"

"Me?" said the youth. "I'm going dancing is what I'm going to do." He pulled out his walkman and prepared to plug up his ear. "What are you going to do?" he asked, needing to be the last one to hurl a challenge.

"Well," said Niall, surprised that the youth even inquired. "I'm leaving home. I'm going out in the world."

"Oh," said the concave one, politely attaching his plug now.

The sprinter was ready for boarding. Niall took his seat. As the train pulled out of the station heading south, he noticed a parade of about fifty placard-waving demonstrators foisting their way through town. "National Day of Action," "Merthyr to Pentrebach,""Don't Shut Down the Old Peoples' Home" were the signs he caught sight of as the train made a motion picture out of the fading town. He hoped they would get their way.

Niall opened up his newspaper now to read the news of the world spread out before him, but he decided it could wait until the town had thoroughly vanished from his view. Things spun by so rapidly out the window that what he was seeing no longer made sense. He wondered about the real meaning of geography and why the world was round.

SMALL WAR IN NUTTER'S MILL

The way some people looked at it was on Thursday you could buy things like New Hampshire butter-and-egg corn, blueberry and strawberry-rhubarb pies, maple syrup, peaches, pears, apples, lettuce, penuche fudge, and geraniums or pink petunias for your window boxes, but on Friday you couldn't. The reason was George Thibedeau took it into his granite head to give it all away.

This caused the biggest stink Nutter's Mill had seen in its over two hundred and fifty year history. People had to take sides immediately. Everybody agreed it had been a long time coming. Still, you can imagine their reaction when they saw that big sign George put up in front of the stand, reading:

FREE
COME AND GET IT. EVERYTHING GOES
GERANIUMS AND VEGETABLES
ALL YOU CAN CARRY

Junie Thibedeau's parents counter-attacked and tried to turn folks against her husband right away. They put up a sign at midnight long after George had gone to sleep with all those beers in his belly, saying:

DON'T DO BUSINESS HERE
THIS MAN IS MEAN TO HIS WIFE

Talk about daring; they put up that sign in front of Nutter's Mill Produce Stand right out on the highway where everybody traveling from Concord and Nashua up to Loon Mountain and beyond could see it, and that stand's been there for over thirty-five years, a fixture, and a place where the locals as well as summer people get many of their vegetables and flowers. In fact, Junie Thibedeau's famous for her homemade pies and fudge. People come from miles around. Rumor has it the whole Hollywood contingent of *On Golden Pond* came over from Squam Lake when they were filming there. Mrs. Richardson swore she saw Katharine Hepburn and Jane Fonda among them, but Junie never confirmed that, only smiled when asked about it.

I don't like to make value judgments on people's behavior. Nobody's perfect, especially Nutter's Mill people, although we won't carry that thought any further, will we? But, frankly, George sends local orneriness right over the dam, in my opinion. It's one thing to make fun of the flatlanders and summer visitors behind their backs, but George has been known to be openly insulting to them right to their faces, especially people from New Jersey, whom he's always lecturing on why do they charge him twenty-five cents every quarter mile on the Garden State Parkway, like they're personally responsible. And he blames all forest fires on New Jersey people claiming they cause them by flicking their cigarettes out the windows of cars as they barrel up to the Flume and the Old Man of the Mountain. Not too many people have ever found George amusing.

Of course, he did work hard. The produce stand was his idea. He and his brother built it, and I have to say it's the best seasonal commercial structure around, long, like a low barn, sturdy, and painted a gleaming white which George keeps up each year. He goes down to Franklin to buy the paint for it at Keegan's, that good Kyanize paint that lasts longer than others. So the place looks inviting, and it's set back from the road with perfect sightlines either way, and plenty of parking spaces in the back. Nothing controversial about it. Only problem, recurring, is someone will complain every so often that the corn comes from New Jersey instead of New Hampshire. George denies smuggling in alien corn, but all the locals know the difference. When our corn comes in it's sweet butter-and-egg and any fool can readily tell the difference. We just don't buy corn before the Fourth of July.

Junie's the real attraction, however. She's a sweet-faced woman with apples in her cheeks, soft brown eyes, and a lot of Mom-appeal about her. If George is an acid-tongued old fart, she's warm and friendly, fussing about the place, watering the plants, checking on who's ordered pies and what kinds and whether George has turned the cooler down to the right temperature. Many feel the recent unpleasantness is the direct result of Junie's being so self-effacing all those years in deference to her husband's fascistic tendencies.

Junie's parents are Rhys and Janet Evans who run the local mortuary in the big town of Shadwell, about eight miles down the road from Nutter's Mill. Junie's their only daughter and they won't take flak off nobody over her. That's why Rhys got out on the road in the dead of night and put up his own inflammatory sign blocking out the one George himself had personally put up, so that the next day all Nutter's Mill knew there was some small war going on at the produce stand, forcing all of us to become instant Arabs and Israelis.

Well, when George woke up the next morning, the first thing he saw when he looked out the window of his house, set back from the road just a little more than the stand, was cars slowing up both ways on the main highway. He wondered what the hell they were slowing up for, and then he spotted his in-laws and Junie out front and he realized all was not so quiet on the New Hampshire front.

Junie carefully explained to anyone who asked that when she had told George she had had enough of his bone-headedness and was planning to divorce him, George reminded her that they owned the business together and that he would make sure she'd never get any alimony out of him. Then, apparently, George in a furious drunken rage, decided he would liquidate the entire stock by giving it away so that Junie's half would fly down the pike along with his, if that's the way it was going to be. Junie guessed he would head for Florida where they spent winters. She said his mean style went over better down there, that he had a lot of nasty friends he played golf with and nobody minded that they tore up the greens.

"I tried, George. I just can't talk to you anymore."

"Making a fool out of me. Get me a beer."

"No. You've had enough."

"Enough of you and your arrogant parents. They put you up to this, didn't they?"

"What'll you do?"

"Go talk to your blasted lawyer. I want the dog, too."

"Mooseminder hates Florida. You know that."

"He loves it. He catches fish."

"Labs don't like warm climates."

"Mooseminder does."

"You can't take him. He stays at the stand."

"Talk to your lawyer. I've nothing further to say to you."

"George, you ruined it all. Don't blame me. I did my best."

"Your best to make a fool out of me, but I'll show you and your parents."

The result of that exchange was George put up his sign giving away freebies to anyone who stopped. Junie drove in from her family's house where she was staying and when she saw what was going on--a regular traffic jam of flatlanders looting the place like it was Los Angeles in a riot--she turned right around and went back to her home where she about cried her heart out. George's showboating made Rhys Evans so mad he put Junie and Janet in his biggest hearse with him and they drove out to the produce stand to set up a picket line with the long black hearse presiding ominously like some finite solid wall of death to anyone who crossed over.

When I first came upon the scene, there were Rhys, Junie, and Janet at the entrance to the driveway trying to turn drivers away, and among the hanging plants, geraniums and petunias under the overhang of the stand, you could see George standing there like some hopped-up Jesus exhorting people to load up their cars with anything they wanted. "It's free," George was screaming. "What're you waiting for. Don't you Yankees know a bargain when it bites you?"

Emma Richardson was helping out the Evanses. You wouldn't have believed her, that tall figure in the flowery dress with the straw hat and dangling earrings whose ambition was to be an Episcopalian priest and whom everybody made fun of because of her pretentious style, standing out there like Joan of Arc of the Highway, waving people back like she was on fire with the Good Lord's work. One thing I'll say: Most of the time our local folks don't traffic much with one another, but when trouble or treason, as in the case of George, flares up, we cluster around one another like Concord minutemen and we fight. "Live Free or Die" is our motto, and we mean business. You've got to be on your guard when you've got Vermont on one side, Maine on the other, and Doowhat youchusetts to your south. Emma Richardson that day personally turned away thirty-four cars.

Only truly greedy people crossed the picket line. Judd Thompson, head of the Democratic party in Shadwell, told me the only locals he saw crossing the line were Republicans, but you can't put too much stock in that. Judd sees Republicans behind every bad idea that comes up around here. Most of the scabs, as far as I could see, were flatlanders. I looked at license plates-- mostly Massachusetts. What can you expect? One New York van screeched in for a dime stop, and I swear those people hauled away enough booty to open up a shop.

The war started on Thursday and lasted through Sunday. Then suddenly there was nothing left at the stand and nobody showed up all day. An uneasy Edward Hopper calm descended on the place. We all drove by to see what was going on, but nothing was. Naturally, you had to be pretty discreet so as not to appear too nosey, but the truth is nobody seemed to know what had happened. One thing was certain, though. George Thibedeau had split because if he were still in town, he would have been out there scrapping away, fighting it out, giving the whole world away in this bravura style he developed in his last-ditch effort.

The Evanses were not in their usual pews in the Congo church on Sunday in Shadwell, either, and since there had been no funerals that Saturday and none coming up that anybody knew about, the best guess was that they had gone down to Concord or Manchester to see about a lawyer.

They didn't return until Tuesday and it turned out gossip had been right. They hired a hotshot Harvard lawyer from Concord who had served divorce papers on George and was untangling the legal problems of the produce stand for them. One rumor had it that the lawyer had contacted N.O.W. and that Gloria Steinem and Betty Friedan had both personally faxed George. So maybe that's what changed the tide.

Emma Richardson, of course, went over to offer the Evanses financial as well as spiritual consolation if they needed it, and she reported that Junie, although thoroughly devastated by the whole experience, had said to her: "I plan to run that stand myself with the help of daddy and mom. I'm trying to perk up, but it's really tough."

Anyway, there's good news in town today. Last night, the letters on the sign got changed again. On one side it reads:

THERE IS LIFE AFTER GEORGE

On the other:

OPENING FRIDAY
WE VALUE OUR FORMER AND NEW CUSTOMERS

We'll all be there. Emma Richardson is going to ride cash register. Rhys Evans is going to be in charge of the freezer and coolers. Janet is overseeing the pies and fudge. I'm planning on playing grocery boy. And Junie is just going to smile her warm, gracious smile and assure everybody that things are going to be just fine now that George and his traitor dog have hightailed it back to Florida.

SINGLETON'S BARN

One minute there was no one there--just the yard, the huge looming green barn and a deepening grey in the sky and trees around us indicating a storm could be hurtling down from behind Mount Seskatenatchee, at whose base our farm was. But when I blinked, there he was, a small figure with long hair, an oddly perched hat that hid his eyes, a mustache and a quizzical smile as though he were some itinerant Arlo Guthrie, half-elf, half-child, left over from an ancient race of Flower Children.

"What do you want?" I shot out at him, as the wind rose and dark clouds lumbered by overhead.

He said nothing, but just continued smiling. An enigma, he approached slowly, walking up the slanting lawn to the house, so that he seemed to get bigger and more real as he approached. He stood in front of me. I looked into his eyes, light hazel, like two beautiful glistening marbles. He couldn't be a threat, could he? I saw his soft, light brown shoulder-length hair curling out from under his grey fedora, his fine features, an aristocratic look about him despite the Irish leprechaun appearance.

"Who are you?" My wife, Rina, joined me, quietly looking out the screen door on the porch. She waited for his answer. There was a moment of odd silence during which it seemed even the birds withdrew their song.

"Lee Singleton," he said in a deep, mature voice, older than his years which seemed to be in his twenties somewhere. He extended his hand and bowed ever so slightly.

I shook his hand. A gentleman then. Clearly not a local with those old-world manners.

"I'm looking for work. I live in Shadwell."

"This is Nutter's Mill," said Rina. "You're on the Sesky Mountain Road. Were you heading up to the lodge?"

"No. I was born right down there." He indicated the bottom of the road, which makes a sharp angle down in the valley just beyond the schoolhouse.

"Singleton?" I said. "Don't know that name."

"My father built that house down there next to the firehouse. I grew up there, but left when I was eight. We went to Maine."

"Jonathan?" asked my wife.

"That was my father."

"But you were only there a short while."

"Nine years."

I laughed. "That's a short time around here. Now that you mention it, I do remember a Jonathan. Didn't know it was Singleton, though."

"It was," Rina said. "Nice man. I remember him clearly. Looks like it's going to storm."

"It'll pass over," said the young man. "It'll shoot over Seskatenatchee from Caanan, but it'll chase down the lake, over to Hebron and up to Loon Mountain and then into Fryburg and Bridgeton in Maine. That's the standard path."

"What can we do for you?" I said.

"I'm a carpenter," the young man said. "Here." He handed me a business card that read:

Lee Singleton
CUSTOM BUILDER--MASTER CARPENTER
RD #2, Shadwell, New Hampshire, 03222
(603) 744-2174

"We need water," Rina said. "That's our big problem at the moment. Do you know anything about wells?

"We think our well's gone dry," I explained, "or just silted up."

"There's a peculiar taste," said Rina. "Moldy, acrid. Something's wrong."

"I put in a deep well at my place," Singleton said. "I built my own house. I can get you water. Where's your well?"

I pointed up into the woods behind the house. "There."

"I'll take a look," he said.

"But it's going to rain," said Rina.

"No problem," he said. "I don't think it will."

I laughed, knowing how whimsical the weather is where we live.

"We're the Williamses," I said, extending my hand in a tentative shake to indicate he shouldn't be so certain about weather predictions. "George and Rina. We're retired teachers from Massachusetts, originally, but now we're here full time."

"If we can afford it," Rina said.

"Pretty expensive place to keep up," I added.

"Tell me about it," the young man said. "And I'm not even near retirement."

"I'll go up to the well with you," I said.

He put out his hand to stop me. "Don't need to. Just point me in the right direction."

"Let's go around back then. It's not far, just in that first grove of trees up the hill."

I took him around back and showed him what I meant.

"Did you see his eyes?" Rina asked me when he was out of sight.

"Incredible."

"I remember Jonathan," she said. "But I don't recall seeing any kids there. Of course, in those days we were just here for two weeks in the summer. I'll ask Lois. She'll know."

"Look at that," I said, indicating a towering shaft of sunlight sweeping over the barn and trees. "It's blown over."

It turned out we not only needed water, we needed a new wellhouse to replace the rotting one Singleton found there when he looked. He also discovered a dead hedgehog floating on the water in the well. "Fell in through the crumbling wood. Who put that cover on it for you?"

"Must have been Alvin," I said. "It's been there for ages."

"Alvin Scandrett?"

"Yes."

"He was my mentor. I hung out at his cabin."

"The hermit of Loosestrife Creek," Rina laughed.

"I learned everything from him," Singleton said. "How to build, how to hunt, how to find water, how to plant."

"Well, what's our problem then?" I asked.

"Your well's too shallow. Either dig a new one or deepen this one and put up a new wellhouse over it."

"This is our third well," explained Rina." We have trouble with it running dry sometimes in July and August, just when people want to come for visits."

"I can dig it deeper," Singleton said. "It's lined with stones, a good old-fashioned New England farm well. Nothing wrong with it basically."

"How much would all that cost?" I asked. "We're not made of money, you know."

"I get twelve dollars an hour for my time, plus materials. I don't waste time. You don't pay for lunch breaks, trips to the lumber yard, or goofing off. I work fast. I take pride in what I do."

"I've often thought we needed a deep well," said Rina. "How expensive would that be?"

"Depends. Need to rent a machine for that. Could get one over in Plymouth like the one I used at my place. It goes by the foot. You're part way up the mountain. Could cost you something."

"Is our well on the best possible site?" I asked. "It seems so far from the house."

"We can find out," Singleton replied. He disappeared into the apple trees and birches at the margin of open land around the house and approached us a few minutes later with a forked branch in his hand, like a huge wishbone. "This is a divining rod," he said. "Do you know how it works?"

"I've heard of them," I told him, "but frankly I'm skeptical."

"Good," he said. "You're just the man we need, Mr. Williams." He handed the branch to me, arranging it in my hands, pointing it outward, as though I were going to use a power mower or push a wheelbarrow. "Now, don't grip it too tightly, just go with the flow, walk over here a bit."

I did what he asked, smiling foolishly at Rina, but suddenly I felt a tug as the apex of the divining rod pointed downward. I hadn't pushed it or done anything unusual. It just seemed to bend down of its own accord.

"There's water down there," he said. "But you wouldn't want to sink your well in that spot since your septic field runs out this way, doesn't it? Let's go round to the back of the house."

At the rear of the house, he indicated the distant grove of trees in which the current well was situated. "If you cross the line that brings the water in," he said, "You should feel the tug downward. Start walking."

I did, and at about eight feet along, I felt the same odd pull on the branch.

"The water pipe is just below you," he explained. "Walk up toward the trees."

I zig-zagged up the hill toward the well, sometimes staying on the water line, sometimes off it. Rina had to try it too. She had the same impression I had. Both of us were exhilarated from this discovery. "My God, it works," I shouted.

"Farmers know a few things," Lee Singleton said with a wry smile.

For that, we gave him the job--to dig out the existing well and build a new little house over it. We would test him further.

A week later during which Singleton had come to our house almost daily, disappearing into the woods with lumber, paint, and tools, seldom stopping to say more than "Morning," or "That's it for today," he stopped by one evening and said, "When you've a mind to, you might want to take a look at the new wellhouse."

"Finished?"

"Yep. Looks pretty good, too. You'll like it. I'll bring over the bill when I add up the cost."

"How much? Ball park?"

"One fifty, I reckon. Somewhere around there. Isn't that what I told you?"

"Yes," said Rina, coming into the scene. "Maybe even less."

"Okay, thanks," I said, watching him square away the flatbed of his pickup. "We'll take a look."

Rina and I went back into the woods to look at the new wellhouse. A solid, perfectly constructed housing over the well, tight, secure, excellent work for hereabouts.

"George, he did a marvelous job," declared Rina. "I think we should have him look at the barn."

"We can't afford it," I replied. "But if he can do work like that, maybe he could give us an estimate or something. "

"I'm worried," said Rina.

"I know. We knew the place would cost a lot."

"But prices keep going up. This was my family's place, really all I inherited from them. I don't know if we can afford it. I think sometimes we've made a mistake."

"Look," I said to her. "I love the place too. Give the boy a chance."

"I want to," she said. "He reminds me of . . . "

"I know. I thought of that too. He is like Jimmy, if he had lived."

When Singleton brought over the bill two days later--it came to one hundred twenty-eight dollars. Rina and I exchanged looks. We could easily afford that. I asked if he'd take a look at the barn.

"What's wrong with it?"

"Well, it's leaning," I said. "We had Jay Pickrell shore it up, but that was ten years ago and he used a thick wire I'm always hitting my head on."

"We think it needs solider reinforcement," said Rina. "My brother said there's powder-post beetle in it. It's old. It goes back to the eighteenth century."

"I'll take a look at it," Singleton said. Rina and I sat out on the porch sipping iced tea while Singleton poked around. We saw him circling the barn several times, looking up at it, holding up a thumb now and then to make a kind of plumb line. He looked like an elf against the huge green behemoth of a barn flanking our trim, white house. Rina offered him a drink when he returned to give us his verdict. "Don't drink," he said. "I work for A.A. now, but I'll take some of that iced tea, thank you."

"Certainly," Rina said. "Now what's your prognostication for the barn?"

Lee Singleton's plan for the rickety barn was a bold one. Nothing less than a complete replacement would do. The old barn was too shaky now and becoming really dangerous. He would have to tear the whole thing down and start from scratch. The new one would look the same, only it would have more room down below for the cars and a larger room upstairs with better headroom and windows that could be screened in to keep the bugs out. He would tear down the old barn, remove the timbers, build the new one and arrange for the electrician if we wanted him to. His price: Fifteen thousand dollars. We would have to think it over.

I remember looking into those unusual eyes to see if he was kidding. The elf-king pulling down our giant barn and building a new one.

"Who would help you?" I asked.

"I'd hire some local guys when I need them," he said, "but I'd probably do most of it myself."

"How can one person do all that?" asked Rina.

"I built my own barn," Lee said. "If you want to take a look at it, I live just over on Jefford's Mill Road. I built an addition to my house, too."

"We'll talk it over," I said, astonished at the will of this young man.

There was plenty to discuss. Fifteen thousand dollars would make a serious inroad to our small savings. Rina worried that it would take years to build up that amount again and we both acknowledged that arthritis was slowing me down and making me dependent on outside help more each year.

Singleton, of course, had proved himself with both of us. We trusted him, but still it was a financial and moral gamble for us. Sometimes when we discussed it, it was almost as though we were discussing Jimmy, our son, who was killed in an accident with a drunk driver back in Weymouth twenty-two years ago.

We had developed such an affection for Singleton now that we ultimately decided to let him go ahead with the project. I wrote out a check for him which he took to the Perrault Brothers Lumber Company to establish his credit. Then he drew against it as he needed supplies.

We watched from the porch as he single-handedly pulled down the old barn. I would go up close to him sometimes to ask if he needed help, as though I could provide any, but Rina had egged me on. I was amazed at how strong he was, the muscles of his sinewy arms taut and glistening as he used his legs as a fulcrum against beams many times his weight. He was like some extraordinary ant who understood just how much tension was needed, just how much give, a perfectly balanced, efficient machine.

From time to time he would come up to us with something discovered.

"Look at this."

Something leathery, a pouch maybe. "What?"

"I found this behind a wall. It's a soldier's case. There's a map in it with 1783 written on it. He must have concealed it in the barn."

"For heaven's sake," said Rina.

"I'd date that barn at around that time," said Lee. "You can tell by the hand-hewn beams. You'll see they marked them with Roman numerals. Your barn has no nails in it, only wooden pegs. But these old beams are worth something. I'm stacking them up on the far side. Somebody might want them, antique dealers or architects."

"I'm amazed," said Rina.

"And I'll tell you something else," said Lee. "You've got snakes in the side walls of the barn."

"What kind?"

"Just garter snakes," said Lee. "Nothing too dangerous. They climb up and snuggle in walls."

Rina laughed. "Well, we have flying squirrels in the attic and bats in the barn. Maybe we'll open up a zoo."

"I chased all the bats out of the barn," Lee said. "I could hear their high-pitched squealing."

"It's looking good," I said. "But are you sure you can do it all yourself?"

"Haven't had any problem yet," he said, with the cocky confidence of the young and able.

Have you ever fallen asleep, dreaming that something was transpiring before your eyes and then awakened only to find it was true--that a plain evergreen ripped from the forest could become a glowing, lighted, magical Christmas tree with presents and warmth and love under it? That's essentially what happened one morning when I woke up late, looked out to see what all the banging was about and found the light wood skeleton of the new barn shining golden and pristine in the sunlight for all the world to see. On top of it was Lee Singleton, the Master Builder, hammering away against the dark green of the pines and the bright blue of the New Hampshire sky.

"Good morning, Lee," I boomed out to him from my upstairs window.

"Morning," his voice came back to me, with a slight tipping of his fedora hat, not missing a beat in his tap-tap-tap. "How do you like it?"

I cupped my hands. "Looks great. I like it fine."

The figure was silhouetted against the sky for a moment. "Still skeptical that I could do it?"

"Nope."

A kid's laugh, high-pitched. A rat-a-tat-tat of confident hammering now. He had made his point.

Rina was full of wonderment. "Will you look at that, George? Isn't he something. Oh, we're going to have so much more room."

Cars began slowing up on the road up to the Appalachian Mountain Lodge on Mt. Seskatenatchee. Drivers wanted to see what glorious new edifice was going up on our property.

"Thought there was a green barn there yesterday," said Skinny Dracott on his way up to the lodge. "Surprised to see this huge structure this morning."

"That's our new barn, Skinny," explained Rina, while Skinny gawked at it out his car window.

"Who's your builder? Looks like a kid."

"Lee Singleton."

"Singleton?" said Skinny. "Oh, well, I hope he'll do a good job."

"He is," I said, joining Rina at the side of the road.

"Looks pretty good," said Skinny. "But Lee has had his problems."

"Not with us," I said.

"No?" said Skinny. "Alcohol and drugs, but I guess

he's okay now."

"He is," I said, annoyed at local labels which last for life on a person around here.

"Gotta be going," said Skinny. "Well, it looks pretty fair, I'll say that. Catch you later." And he gunned his car up the road toward his lackey job as the handyman-waiter at the lodge.

"There's always somebody waiting to spoil everybody's fun around here," I said to Rina. "That's the local disease."

Rina smiled tolerantly, and then turned to look at the erector set barn taking shape on the lawn. "Well, I love it," she said. "I think he's a miracle worker."

The barn shone beautifully through the early days of May in New Hampshire. Its golden bones gradually got painted from the top down in soaking tones of bright green which we all knew would blend into the wood within a few months and settle down to the appropriate blue-green weathered New England barn look. Lee outlined the windows and the doors for the garage underneath with bright white, so that the whole edifice looked like a cover that might have been designed for the ritzy *Architectural Digest*. Both Rina and I were so pleased with the spectactular results that we decided we had to have a party to celebrate the great event, so we simply invited everyone we had ever said hello to for miles around. To our surprise, many people accepted, and some brought people visiting them whom we had never met before. We placed Lee Singleton in the star position as the architect, historian, and master builder that he was and gave him full credit for the wonders he had wrought. But the neighbors treated him with high disdain, I felt.

During the evening, Lee went down into our basement with Rina to retrieve for the party some bottles of wine and cider which we had stored in our wine cellar. He noticed that we had encouraged dry rot by walling in the wine cellar with plastic hangings and he showed us how dangerously the whole main house was balanced. Before the evening was over, we had agreed to another twelve thousand dollars to him to shore up the house with new beams and posts to rid us of the dreaded rot. He would also waterproof the walls, insulate the ceilings, and lay gravel on the earthen basement floor. Rina was upset with the verdict, because this took us to the end of our money, but I said what did she think would become of any house as old as ours? So we both reluctantly agreed and told Lee to go ahead with this new project. That night I broke out in a cold sweat in my sleep.

The next day the whole town was buzzing with news of our barn-raising party, the social event of the year, as though we were a couple of Rockefellers. But while we were getting credit for being clever and resourceful, the true creator, Lee Singleton, was being reviled for having cheated us.

Jay Osborn was quoted as saying the new barn was built of cheap wood and in a bad design. Les Unger said he could have built it for less and put a tin roof on top instead of asphalt shingles to match the other barn. The Dellacort brothers claimed Lee gave us a good price just so he could get back into the good graces of people in town he had previously offended. They said he was an alcoholic and a drugged-out hippie who didn't deserve a break like this.

The Seligman family gave their seal of disapproval by not coming to our party at all. "Big deal," as I said to Rina. "What do you expect of Long Island people anyway?" But what I privately thought is maybe we made a foolish mistake.

Through all the trouble, we were confronted everyday by the seemingly honest, marble-like eyes of Lee Singleton, who alone moved our basement timbers, sending huge earthquake-like vibrations up into the living room and dining room and downstairs bedroom so that we had to retreat to the kitchen or back porch for safety.

"What the hell are you doing, Lee?" I would shout.

"Saving your house," he would say. "Renewing your timbers."

"All right," Rina would say. "But enough of this thundering." I thought at one point that she might have a nervous breakdown. Although we no longer mentioned it, I think she had begun to feel we had been taken in by an artful con artist.

Mercifully, it took only a week and a half and then we were on solid ground again in our living room.

The basement now was dry and secure, well supported with new beams, gravel, and white walls where once everything had been dark and dank. The plastic hangings were pulled down. The wine cellar was no more. "You will have to drink Coke," pronounced Singleton.

Lee Singleton faded out of our lives at that point. He had done his job admirably, we thought, and deserved a rest and a respite from us, and we from him, since we were at the end of the line financially and uncertain about our future. About two weeks later, though, Skinny Dracott pulled his car up to our fence bordering the road when he spotted us working in the garden. "Looks like you lost your carpenter," he said to Rina, who reached him before I did.

"What do you mean?"

"I mean I heard he's gone back to Maine."

I joined them, catching their drift. "How come?"

"Folks around here ain't fooled by Lee Singleton. He lost his father's money, he got too big for his britches, and there's nobody really wants to hire him except you."

I was angry. "What do you mean by that?"

"Nothing. It just seems he really latched on to a good thing with you folks and now he's taken it all and run."

"He helped us greatly," said Rina. "Look at that barn. Look at our house with its dry basement."

"Oh, well, you suit yourself," said Skinny starting up his car. "You can afford it. Most of us can't. We don't have that kind of money to throw around."

"No, you'd prefer to blow it all in Disney World in Florida every winter," I shot at him, angry at this display of bitchy provincialism.

"Listen, George, you're the one that paid for the kid, not me," said Skinny. "If you're satisfied, that's all that matters, ain't it?"

"That's right," I said, "and if you've finished your bad-mouthing, the lodge is calling you to get your ass up the hill to wait on those flatlanders. So, scat."

As the locals might put it, "I like to tell you, Skinny Dracott hot-rodded his fucking buggy up the road to the lodge."

Rina and I sit on our porch in the long summer twilights now, swatting flies and mosquitoes, drinking iced tea and thinking what a fine new barn we have. We've convinced ourselves we did the right thing.

Social security and my teaching pension are coming in okay, building up slowly again.

We miss Lee Singleton, wonder what he's doing now over in the state of Maine, wish him well, remember his astonishing powers, his particular magic, and his transformation of our place into something solid, useful, and beautiful.

We think of him almost as the son we lost, although it remains only a hidden thought with us. We never verbalize it.

We never discuss Lee with our neighbors, whose brains are the purest granite anyone will ever find in the entire state of New Hampshire. They've locked him out of their minds completely as a loser and undesirable, but we've taken him into ours as a hero and artist.

So we win.

SHOES

The stringy woman with the leathery hands fixed me with her steel blue eyes before she said anything else at lunch and shot-gunned, "We couldn't go into Australia because of the storm, so I decided to have a ball in New Zealand. I went bungee-jumping for the first time. I'm eighty-three and I think I'm doing pretty darn well for it."

"I'd say you were."

The woman looked startled, "Oh, you're not who I think you are." She turned toward the waiter who was out of her reach attending to other passengers just sliding into their chairs in the Orleans Room on the steamboat.

"It's okay," I said. "It's open seating at lunch."

"I know that," she replied, snapping those cold eyes at me again. "I see that I'm one table off. I usually sit at that place, but there are different people there now."

"I'm Robert Saunders," I said. "Cincinnati."

"Betty Hallam," she replied. "Arizona." She hauled in a waiter now. "I'd like the creole crabcakes, a glass of iced tea, and we'll talk about the dessert later." I noticed that she wore no makeup, earrings, or jewelry of any kind. She had a kind of frank, honest face, like an eighty-three year old Martina Navratilovna, very trim and fit, and obviously traveling alone.

"Have you been on the *Delta Queen* before?" I asked, almost expecting a routine "yes" because so many of the passengers were repeaters.

"No," she said. "I'm just back from Australia. Well, as I told you, we didn't get there exactly. There was that big storm, you know."

"What ship were you on?"

"Oh, that Dutch ship. What's its name?"

"The Holland-America line?"

"Yes."

"The *Rotterdam*?"

"That's the one."

"That must have been nice."

"Well, it wasn't. I've never seen such a storm. Everybody was sick."

"How long did it take?"

"Over a month. Much too long. I don't like spending that length of time at sea. I went alone. I had taken my grandson to Alaska last year. He's twelve. He was very excited about the trip, told everybody not to give him presents for his birthday which came just before we left. Said he was going to take the money and buy gifts for everybody when he got there."

"That was unusually considerate, wasn't it?"

"That's what I thought at first."

"What happened?"

"They've got those damn video arcades on board. He spent all his time and all his money playing those things. The captain's voice came over the loudspeaker once saying he had spotted a school of dolphins and that the passengers might like to have a look. I went into that video room and told Jason I thought this was something he should see-- something educational and unusual, you know, and you know what he said to me?"

"No."

"He said, 'I've seen them before.' 'Where?' I asked him. 'On tv,' he replied. 'Well, this is different,' I said. 'I think you should go out on deck to see them for yourself.' Do you know what that fresh kid said? He said, 'I don't have to take orders from you.' 'Who says?' I challenged him. 'My mother,' he said. 'She said I didn't have to mind you.' Well, I was so mad when I heard that--If my daughter had said something like that to him. And do you know what? When we got back to Los Angeles, I told her what he had said and she said, 'That's right. I told him that.' Can you believe it? That damned kid won't go on any more trips with me. That's the way they're bringing up children today. So I just go by myself, and I'm having a fine time without either of them. If that's the way they want to live, so be it, I say."

The waiter placed the crabcakes in front of her. "Good," she said, taking a bite. "Don't forget my iced tea. What do you do?" she asked me.

"I was an editor for a business publication," I replied. "But I'm taking the *Delta Queen* down the Mississippi to New Orleans as a kind of retirement present to myself."

She looked surprised. "Are you old enough to retire?" she laughed.

"Fifty-five," I said. "I'm taking early retirement."

"God," she said. "I couldn't think of quitting."

"What do you do?"

"I work with the Hopi Indians."

"Doing what?"

"Everything. I taught them how to read and write English. I taught them how to make shoes."

"Didn't they know how?"

"Hell, no. They slopped around on the hot sand, and you know it can get plenty cold at night. The desert runs to extremes in temperature."

"How did you learn about making shoes?"

"From the Girl Scouts in Connecticut, that's where. It's very easy. You take those carpet samples, you know. Sometimes they'll even give them to you free, and then you cut them across and staple them on to a slab of leather. That makes a carpet shoe. Well, I taught them how to do that, and they're in the business now. They all wear them."

"How'd that all come about?"

"They were good to me. They gave me a house."

"A house?"

"Oh, it's a long story. You don't want to hear it." She hailed the waiter. "Would you please give me some attention? I'd like some more iced tea."

I didn't see Betty much after that. I'd hear her, just at my back, sitting at her table during dinner, sometimes driving the conversation, sometimes oddly quiet throughout the meal. I saw her once after dinner when she looked into the bar where there was all sorts of banjo-thumping, hooting, and hollering going on, but she gave a quick look of disgust and no sign at all that she recognized me. So I assumed the deep freeze was on. I had displeased her in some way, probably by being at the table she was forced to sit at and so she blamed me for the whole deal.

It didn't matter much to me. I wasn't on the boat to meet people. I was there to float down the Mississippi gracefully, not exactly on a raft like Huckleberry Finn, but the next best thing to it--an authentic sternwheeler built in 1927--and the people I most wanted to get to know were the captain, the crew, and the townspeople we'd see along the levees at the places we stopped, exotic places like Natchez, St. Francisville, and Vicksburg. I wanted to feel the pulse of the river flow through me and absorb as much as I could of the atmosphere of the deep South.

Lazy days, winding days, twisting and turning--I had no idea the Mississippi between Memphis and New Orleans could make so many angular turns. The Captain told me how difficult it was to be a river pilot. I could believe it. Flat barges, often as many as twenty-five or thirty, were pushed by a single towboat downstream. They'd glide by like giant alligators in the swift current of the muddy, roiled-up river. Mornings, evenings, I'd sit on the deck and watch the low gray-brown landscape with its cottonwood and willow trees and birds circling lazily high above. At each new levee I'd observe the skilled crewmen throwing out lines, tying them around available trees and swinging out the stage from the bow of the ship to make a gangplank for passengers and crew to go ashore. Betty Hallam was not much on my mind. Only occasionally would I catch a glimpse of her scurrying ashore with what seemed to be amazing alacrity for someone her age. But what else was new?

Some excitement on board. We were going to land at a big city--Baton Rouge, the capital of Louisiana. For the first time, we pulled up to a proper pier, this one several levels tall to allow for the tremendous flooding that occurs on the Mississippi, the concrete pier topped off by what looked like giant paper clips, clearly the result of the architect's feverish imagination. I found myself standing next to Betty Hallam as a line of passengers formed to disembark. "Hello, Betty," I said.

"What?"

"Good morning. You're not taking the tour?"

"No. I'm going on my own. I've got to buy shoes. The ones I brought with me are killing me."

"Do you want me to help you? I could go with you."

"No, thank you. I know just what to do. The purser gave me the address and the direction."

"Okay."

"Thank you. What's your name?"

"Robert Saunders."

"Yes, that's right. See you later."

She disappeared through the first batch of people ashore. We had to go over a long concrete path and then up over a bridge that crossed a road before being dumped into downtown Baton Rouge.

I spent the day in the city seeing the old state capital, the new state capital, the university, and walking through an art gallery. It was hot and humid with the flash of an approaching thunderstorm in the air as I walked back to the boat around 5:00 p.m. Just ahead of me, barely dragging herself along, I caught sight of Betty, toting two large shopping bags. "Betty?" I called.

She stopped, turned around, looking half-grateful in her weariness for this intrusion into her blurred, numbed thought process. "Oh, hello," she replied. "Been shopping." She held up one of the white plastic bags as proof.

I grabbed it from her. "Here, let me help you." To my surprise, she also handed me the other one. "Be careful. I've got shoes and sneakers in there."

"So you found the store all right?"

"I found it, yes, but I got lost, went around the block twice, walking right by it. I tried to find a taxi, but couldn't. I can't understand anything these people say."

We were at the ship now. "Do you want a coke or something?"

"No, thanks," she said. "But a glass of iced tea would look plenty good. God, I'm ready to drop."

Good idea, so we both fell into chairs in the forward saloon and ordered our cool drinks.

"What happened is that I was born in Connecticut, grew up there, went to school, had these terrible sinus headaches all my life. Then I got married. We had our daughter, bought a nice house. But I went out to visit a friend in Arizona one spring, and, I couldn't believe it, I never felt better in my life. So I called my husband, said, 'Sell, the house, bring the dog and the child, and come out here.' And he did, and I never went back. I guess that dry, desert climate was just the thing for my head. Cleared up all my problems. My mother called and said, 'Betty, what's this I hear about your quitting Connecticut for Arizona?' And I said, 'Pack your bags, mama. You'll love this place.' So she did, and she did, but then she discovered California and ended up in Palm Springs for the rest of her life. Westward, ho, huh?'"

"You said you work with the Hopi Indians."

"I used to go there to help them, still do. You know, their reservation is quite far out, about an hour and a half away. Well, when Bob was away on business, I'd take my daughter with me, and I got in the habit of spending the night in the car under those amazing stars instead of driving home all the time. Once, when Marcy was about ten, I think, we were sound asleep in the car and I woke up at dawn to find the medicine man and the chief pounding on the window for me to open up the car. Marcy and I were scared to death, but the chief explained that he wanted to give us a house."

"'A house? What for?' I asked him."

"'To live in,' he replied. 'This house is no longer used. It is contaminated.'"

"The chief said that if a person has died there, the Hopi consider it a bad omen, and no Hopi will ever dwell there again. He claimed three people had died as a result of living in that house. He said that since white people didn't seem to share that belief, perhaps they could inhabit it without harm, and, besides, I looked as though I needed a house since I was sleeping in the car with my child."

"In return, I taught them how to read and write English and I started them on their way to making carpet shoes."

I looked at Betty, astonished at the resilience of this transplanted Easterner. "But what about your other house and your husband?"

"Well, we had two houses for a while, but then Bob and I got divorced. He moved up to Nevada, so I sold our house and lived in the one on the reservation." She laughed. "But I never had any bad luck, despite the Medicine Man."

"What do you mean?"

"Oh, he said something about whoever lives in that house will never know rest, but go round and round and never be happy. The usual hogwash. Imagine. Listen, I've talked too much. I'm pooped. I need to take a nap. See you later." With that, she got up, gathered up her packages and strode off toward her stateroom.

The New Orleans airport waiting room was fairly empty. I had gotten there early because I wanted to be sure of catching my flight back to Cincinnati. I recognized one or two other people there as also having been passengers on the *Delta Queen*. I sat facing the glass doors where the taxis discharged new arrivals. Suddenly, a yellow cab pulled up and out stepped Betty. She needed help with her suitcase, so I opened the door to help her.

"Oh, thanks," she said. "Where do I go from here?"

"The information desk. There was someone there a few minutes ago."

Betty looked around. "Do me a favor?" she asked, showing me her ticket envelope. "Just look at my ticket and tell me if I'm in the right place. What's the airline?"

I looked at her ticket. "Yes," I said. "Delta to Atlanta, then to Phoenix."

"Atlanta? Why are they sending me there?"

"You change," I said. "Isn't that Delta's headquarters?"

"Don't know. What time do I get to Phoenix?"

I looked closely. "8:45," I said.

"Is that this time or Phoenix's time?"

"Phoenix's."

A uniformed woman now appeared in the information booth.

"Someone's there. Thanks very much." Betty lugged her suitcase over toward the desk and I could hear the low drone as she talked with the woman.

I dozed off for a while, hoping the thunderstorm that had been brewing would not hit. I heard the comforting buzz of more people around me now, the staccato flight calls over the loudspeaker system. Suddenly, familiar numbers. I awoke with a start, looked at my watch. My flight was being called. I gathered up my carry-ons, headed toward the gate.

As I looked around, I saw Betty slumped over now in her seat in a kind of deep daydream near her suitcase on the floor in front of her. I hesitated to disturb her, but saw that her eyes were staring straight ahead, so I felt I should say something. "Goodbye," I said. "Good luck." There was no response, just the merest flicker of a smile as she apparently wondered who I was.

I looked back at her just as I passed through the door in time to see her pulling out a shiny new shoe from the suitcase and hold it out in front of her at arm's length, preparatory to putting it on. A woman sitting across from her, reached out, and seemed about to speak.

TRYLONS AND PERISPHERES

I can't walk into this room without noticing that photo. I don't think it is because of the photo itself, which looks like any other 5 X 7 enlargement of a snapshot set in a silver frame, but it is because the lamp, which is on the round table on which the photo is in that dark corner of the living room, is so offensive--a lamp base with a high gloss simulating a vase of flowers--that it attracts my attention and then forces me once again to confront this photo.

I am always drawn to this photo against my will. When I enter this sunken living room with its pattern of light corners and dark corners, I often go over to the chair near this table, turn on the American Beauty lamp and let its sunny glow fall down over the photo into which I can easily stare and get lost in for a few seconds, which expand into a few years, projecting me back into the past where I see in an unnecessarily clear light everything that I am and once was.

The photo apparently was taken on a very sunny day in 1939 or 1940, probably in the spring. It shows Ike, Mooch, and Third standing in front of the Trylon and Perisphere at the New York World's Fair. They are all in their thirties, I would guess. Mooch is standing on the left, tall, conservatively dressed in a double-breasted, pin-striped navy blue suit, probably from Wanamaker's. Mooch was always loyal to his Philadelphia upbringing. He looks a lot like the movie star Joel McCrea in the photo. He has those same very light blue eyes that draw you in even though you don't quite understand what you are seeing.

Ike is in the middle, dressed in a Scottish velvet
jacket with a plaid skirt and a little velvet tam o'shanter on
her head. She stands in her characteristically slightly pigeon-
toed way. Somewhere or other Ike got the idea that it was
cute for a woman to stand pigeon-toed. Maybe she picked it
up from the old Mary Pickford movies of her youth or
something. Most of the snapshots of her in the '20s, '30s,
'40s, and even the '50s show her standing in this manner. She
is smiling in the photo, really almost laughing. She looks like
Loretta Young.

Third is Ike's husband. His real name is George, but
he is George III, like a King of England or France, and
everyone calls him simply "Third" to distinguish him from
his father and grandfather, both of whom are alive and active
in the social ramble. Third looks like William Holden in
Golden Boy or *Our Town*. There is a kind of blond quality
about his face and hair.

Two things you may have noticed: Everybody has a
nickname and everybody looks like a movie star. I don't
know why that is, but that's the way it was back then. Oh, yes,
Gac is not in the photo. Gac is my mother. I think she
probably took the snapshot. And what a good shot it was--
clear, strong contrasts, probably taken on a simple Kodak
box camera. Gac, or *The* Gac, as Dude refers to her, looks
somewhat like Vivien Leigh--or so my aunt, who was a movie
actress herself, says. My aunt looked like Eleanor Lambert
because that's who she actually was.

Nicknames: Imagine my poor father going through
life being called Mooch. Mooch wasn't his name at all, and my
grandmother would cut dead anyone who dared refer to him
by that name in her presence. She hated all nicknames and
also chewing gum and all those others things she said
common people did. I think she thought of us as uncommon
people. She certainly wasn't anybody's run-of-the-mill
grandmother, I'll say that for her, but she couldn't help it.
Her mother was English. My father's real name was Jarvis.
She would name him that! Ike was the one who first called

him Mooch. I wonder if he used to mooch cigarettes from her. She and my father smoked more cigarettes than any people I know. They were directly responsible for my trying cigars when I was eight. I thought it was smart and grown up, and I decided I'd better get started being like them as soon as possible. They were the two people I most admired in my young days.

Ike was so good at smoking cigarettes that she used to sit at the dinner table, draw in smoke, eat a few mouthfuls of food, and then deftly expel the smoke. My sister and I watched her incredulously. "Please have a cigarette," my sister would say innocently to Ike at table and then nudge me with her elbow to watch the results. The Ike Smoking Show was impressive. Even Ike seemed to revel in her unusual talent to draw smoke deep inside her and puff it out in a brilliant stream at a later time.

Ike was my mother's sister. Her real name was Iona, named for some island off the coast of Scotland, but my uncle Chaz said he couldn't stand poetic or geographical names, and he called her Ike, which stuck, because for a long time she worked for Chaz, and so everybody at business called her Ike. Of all my uncles and aunts, she was the only one who had not yet gotten married at the time I began noticing my relatives as interesting people. I think Ike must have been a kind of F. Scott Fitzgerald character in her flaming youth. She was immensely popular, had lots of men buzzing around her all the time, and she was so even-tempered that she never caused trouble or complained. She could do everything--sports especially, tennis, jogging around the track, taking you to the circus, the movies, out to dances, tell you about everything she did, everything she saw.

But there was a sad side to Ike, also. She was engaged for about seven years to a really nice man named Tim. He looked like Cary Grant, so you know how good-looking he was. But he had tuberculosis and was in and out of hospitals a lot during the 1930s. Sometimes Ike would come home from the hospital and you could tell she had been crying because of Tim's condition. Tim was the focus of her life until one night my father brought Third home from the office to dinner, and then the long process began in which she switched over to Third from Tim, and then finally one day Tim was out of her life altogether and she was marrying Third.

I remember the wedding day well because my brother, sister, and I wanted to go to the wedding, but children weren't allowed, so we couldn't. There wasn't room in the rectory. We had to stay at home and wait for reports from the battlefield when Gac and Mooch came home. They reported that the priest was mean, probably because Ike was a Protestant, and actually stopped in the middle of the ceremony to ask her what her name was. Gac said all during the ceremony someone was rattling dishes in a kitchen just off the rectory. "Probably the Holy Ghost," quipped Mooch.

You may have noticed that I called my parents Gac and Mooch. Why not? All their friends did. So did my friends. The only ones who objected were my stuffy old grandmother, some prune-whip schoolteachers, and my uncle Chaz who said flat out that I ought to be shipped off to military school to get me into shape. But I was saved by my grandmother who always automatically vetoed anything Chaz said. My grandmother claimed my lack of principles came from my mother's shanty Irish side of the family. I didn't really care. My mother and father seemed to enjoy being Gac and Mooch to us children, so, bugger off, Britannia.

Ike and Third. No, Ike and Tim. Ike and Tim certainly. They came first. What a wonderful couple of immortal lovers they were to my young mind. Tim would come calling in his little old Chevy that had a rumble seat. Sometimes I would ride with them, bucking the wind in the rumble seat, zooming along at eighteen miles an hour along the shore road to the beach. They both loved the water and were good swimmers. They would hold my hands, and with me in the middle, we would jump over the waves. We must have jumped over the entire Atlantic Ocean at some point in our excursions. The crashing sounds of the foaming surf, the squishy sand, running back up the beach from advancing tides--these were all an integral part of my relationship with them.

Not to mention picnics on the beach complete with bonfires and salt water taffy. Or picnics in parks, on cool lawns under tall shade trees near where people played golf. Straw boaters, blazers, red and white checked table cloths, wicker picnic hampers, Ovaltine, white flannel trousers, and I, a small sprout, running wild around them while they tried to steal a few romantic moments together, never begrudging me my pushiness, finding me funny and amusing. Ike was always laughing and when she laughed full tilt, you had to laugh also. She found the world very funny often and so did I. We would seek out really funny things wherever we went. I think Ike and Tim really loved children. I know I really loved them, and I think it was one of the saddest times in my life when I realized that Tim would never be in our lives again.

And Tim wasn't for the longest time. Tall, lanky, with those handsome Cary Grant looks, I never saw him again until one day in the 1940s after we were in the war and a knock came at the door, which Gac answered, and there was Tim with his wife, and he said hello to me and asked about Ike, who was not there, and then he went away again and later we heard that he had died of tuberculosis after all, and I thought how tragic and unjust it was that such a wonderful person should have been struck off the face of the earth so young.

But Ike survived and she married Third, and in this photo I think they had been married for probably three or four months. Both Ike and Third are superbly dressed, so neat and spiffy at the World's Fair. Mooch always maintained that Third taught Ike neatness. He said Ike was not naturally neat, but that Third, who came from a large family, was used to having everything done with large-family perfection.

There is a little reserve between Ike and Third in the photo. They don't look like lovebirds exactly. There is not that breezy informality that we had with Tim. Maybe it's the occasion or just the time of day. After all, the World's Fair. Some big deal.

Both men in the photo have hats, fedoras. Mooch wears his on his head. Third carries his in his hand. He is dressed in a tan gabardine suit. Very expensive, I'm sure. Third and his father were always fashion-plates. They shopped at Rogers Peet a lot. They liked it better than Brooks Brothers or John David. Third and his father specialized in English foulard ties. When I got to be a teenager both would send over their old ties, suits, and jackets to be made over into new outfits for me. I was the sharpest dresser around for a period in my life.

I am not in the photo, but I am there. At one time I thought I had actually taken this photo, maybe because I have scrutinized it so long and so often in different periods of my life that I began to believe I had to have taken it. But Gac says she actually took the photo, even though I was there with her on that day.

What was I doing, I wonder? I mean at that precise moment. I was probably gathering up more information or sorting through all the pamphlets I already had. I made a huge scrapbook of the World's Fair. It was all I could think of for a long time. We went back to it time and again, maybe a dozen times in all. There was probably not a single pavilion that I missed. I learned so much about Italy, the Soviet Union, France, and all the states--especially Ohio, Missouri, and Pennsylvania, which had the most interesting displays, I thought, and I gathered it all up into a monster scrapbook for which I wrote a commentary. Later, the whole book was displayed in some giant exhibition of students' work at my school. Gac and Mooch loved my scrapbook and took me back to the Fair whenever I wanted to go. It became a joke. I seemed never to get enough of it. I wanted to stop the clock right then and there and freeze the world forever at the World's Fair of 1939.

I saw my first television at the Fair; in fact I was on television there. That was one of its big attractions. You could see a little blue-and-white flickering version of yourself in the World of Tomorrow. And there was a Fountain of Nations there, spurting up huge gushes of water into the air with colored lights playing on them. And operas like *Rigoletto* and *La Traviata* performed by puppets prancing on little tracks in a tiny theatre in the House of Jewels. And an enormous parachute jump that shot you way up into the sky over Flushing Meadow and then dropped you down so fast you'd swear you had just jumped out of an airplane.

I remember all of this. I examine this photograph carefully to scoop it all up. I can almost see the young green grass planted everywhere and the spacious walks and vistas leading up to the pavilions, especially the impressive Soviet Pavilion and the Italian Pavilion with waterfalls coursing down its front. Everything was bright orange and blue, and there were trash containers placed everywhere. There was an order and a pleasing pattern in the design of things. There seemed to be a reason for it all. Queen Elizabeth and King George VI came over from England for it. Mike Todd presented *The Streets of Paris* with Gypsy Rose Lee and Bobby Clark. This was some show to a young kid like me. This was some world. That was some dazzling ride into the World of the Future in the General Motors Pavilion.

What do Mooch, Ike, and Third see? Why are Mooch's eyes shaded by the brim of his hat so that I cannot tell exactly what his expression is? He seems to be looking into the distance. He is not looking at Gac and me. He sees something way beyond us. Does it amuse him? He does have the trace of a smile on his lips. Ike, of course, is looking right at us and smiling. I think Mooch must have said something funny to her. She is looking directly at us as though to say, "Did you hear what that terrible Mooch just said?" I expect she will break into a great gale of laughter just after this photo is taken.

Third is looking a little to the right of us. What was behind us? He's not exactly smiling; there is more a look of tolerant bemusement on his part. Perhaps some passerby is staring a little at the three people posing so perfectly for their photo at the Fair. Perhaps he is suffering their solicitous glances in his direction like some upwardly mobile William Holden who should really be off doing things more suited to one of his station and destiny.

All this took place over fifty years ago. It all came and went, didn't it? Now when you go past Flushing Meadow or near it on the Belt Parkway or Grand Central Parkway all you get is a leftover New York State Pavilion, some relics from a later world's fair, and a big gladiatorial emporium called Shea Stadium. Gac, Mooch, Ike, and Third are all gone now, and I guess I am the only one left on earth now who knows their story, who can identify the happy threesome in the photo in the silver frame.

But my real secret is that I know the ironic endings to all their stories, so that when I look at this photo now I am like an annoying, picky, analytic historian who knows too much. I feel quite certain that succeeding generations will value the silver frame highly and discard with amusement the photo of these people wearing such strange, old-fashioned costumes. Maybe they were lucky, after all, not to have survived into the World of Tomorrow.

PARACHUTE

Maud went into the oven about ten o'clock in the morning. The Gac trussed her up with some good strong cord, stuck a few sharp skewers into her and shoved her in. Then Gac, Ike, Dude, Maggie, and Mooch roared with laughter, grabbed the picnic hampers, the beach umbrellas, the beach blankets, and all of us kids and piled us into the station wagon and the Chevy roadster to go off to the beach while Maud burned.

"We can't take too much time at the beach," warned the Gac, "because the D.D. will be arriving around four and Maud should be done by then." Again, shrieks of hilarity from everybody. The very mention of Maud's name brought on instant laughing madness. I could never figure out just why.

You may have noticed all these strange nicknames at our house. Nothing is what it seems, ever, if you ask me. It is 1939 and you'd think we would have advanced some. People are "snappy dressers" and "swell personalities" and never go by their own names. Gac and Mooch, for instance, are my mother and father, believe it or not. Translation: Gac equals Glenna and Mooch equals Jarvis. Don't ask me why. Ike and Dude are my mother's sister and brother. Translation: Ike equals Iona; Dude equals Wallace. Maggie is Dude's wife. My sister Laurie is twelve, I am ten, and Skeezix is three, just a little creature. He fell out of a tree he wasn't supposed to play in the other day, and when my mother asked him why, he told her that a bird kicked him. That's the way Skeezix is. Not very bright, if you ask me.

Gac, Dude, Ike, and Maggie are all Scottish. Their name is MacGooligan although Maggie was born a Stewart in Scotland. All the MacGooligans are quite fierce. Dude told me the MacGooligans were feared all over Scotland. I can believe it. They scare me when they get going, all together, drinking Scotch and playing poker. Dude said that in the old days the MacGooligans ruled all Scotland and that even the Campbells and MacDonalds ran the other way whenever a MacGooligan came into view. Dude likes boats and anything about the ocean. Gac likes clams, crabs, and all kinds of fish. She eats these things raw. I don't know how she can stand it. Sometimes she makes finnan haddie and stinks up the whole house with it. God, it smells awful. My sister, brother, and I never feel very hungry when we know that's what's for dinner.

Maggie has blonde hair, blue eyes, but no eyebrows. My sister and I look to see if she is growing any, but there is just a blondness there. No eyebrows. She laughs a lot and is a good story teller.

Mooch, my father, is quiet, of Welsh background, but he says funny things to us kids. I don't think the others hear him. He is a very strong swimmer, but the only thing is he can't see without his glasses, so he just strikes out and swims in a straight line. We all stand on the shore shouting at him to stop. He swims halfway to Wales before you can stop him.

I am still afraid of the ocean. It's too rough. I don't really like having the wind knocked out of me. What fun is it to come tumbling into the shore all scrambled up, feet first? Skeezix won't even go near the water. He's smart in this respect, I think. Laurie, of course, is everybody's pet. They call her a regular water rat. She prides herself on being the first one into the ocean and the last out. She eats ice cream the same way--always has to be last. Laurie got all the looks in the family, thank God, they all say. About me, they always poke me in the ribs and say, "Needs fattening up a little. Get some meat on those bones." I say, no thanks, I don't want to be fat. I can get through some narrow places nobody else can.

At the beach we set up two umbrellas. Dude calls it making camp. Maggie, Gac, Mooch, Dude, and I all have red or blond hair and freckled skins. We have to put on lots of oil and sit under the umbrellas. Ike and Laurie are brunettes and get nice tans. They actually lie out in the sun inviting it to dare to burn them. Skeezix, we don't know what he does--tan or burn--because he's got a bald dome with a few strands of blond hair like a ratty bird's nest and he runs around all the time anyway. You can't keep him still. Once he brought back a horseshoe crab that looked like somebody's leather helmet.

Mooch and Dude play catch. Sometimes Ike plays with them. On very crowded days, they have to move back up the beach a bit. Mooch has really big muscles in his arms. He can pump them up so that they look like pillows. Sometimes, on the beach he still lets me lay my head on his bicep, and I fall fast asleep. I do like these beach parties, but I always get tired. Gac says it is the salt air that does this to me. Sometimes it makes it hard for me to breathe too. I have to take in short little gasps of air, otherwise I get sharp pains in my ribs.

Aren't people funny walking up and down on the beach? They wear the strangest bathing suits. Dude has got on those long woolen trunks. They make him look bowlegged, I think. Maggie has on something that I don't know how she can swim in it. You can see right down her chest. It looks like two big mountains to me. Ike is wearing a one-piece shiny blue suit that shimmers like turquoise. She has a good figure, I think, and I can tell all the men on the beach think so, too.

I wear these baggy trunks that slide down around my hips unless I tighten up the drawstring every minute. I always have to wear a long-sleeved shirt over everything to keep the sun away. Laurie wears this two-piece outfit she made my mother pay twenty-five dollars for. I think it looks ridiculous. She thinks she's so grown up because she can swim and dive and won a medal at the country club's swimming meet last summer. Skeezix wears an old pair of my trunks. He doesn't really care. Sometimes he just dashes down the beach with nothing on at all. Some people think it is cute. I think it is just Skeezix being stupid as usual.

We've been here long enough, I think. I went in the water twice. It was low tide, so I could jump over some of the waves, and none of them knocked me down. But my teeth are chattering. Dude asked me if I were cold, and I told him no, but he put his big beach towel around me anyway and that did make me feel warmer for a minute. I can actually hear my teeth knocking together. I can't help it. My arms and legs have gooseflesh all over them. That's what I hate about being skinny.

Finally, Gac says it is time to go, and we gather up everything, including half the sand on the beach and we head back to the cars. Skeezix yells out, "Goodbye, Sahara."

"Time to tackle the D.D.," says Gac, and everybody once again hoots. I don't think the D.D. is any laughing matter.

The D.D. is Douglas Duncan MacGooligan, their cousin from Scotland. My mother said he came over for a visit one summer and has been here ever since. He lived in our house for seven years in the maid's quarters over the garage when we didn't have a maid and when Ike was not yet living with us. But a couple of years ago the D.D. got a permanent job and a place in the city, so he lives there now, thank God. He is quite a sight. He looks like any other bald man who wears glasses, but he wears the MacGooligan kilt around a lot of the time and makes a spectacle out of himself. If you go out with him anywhere, he always manages to get people talking to him, and he's got this weird accent that you have to listen to closely in order to understand. He and I don't exactly get along. He came after me once with a rolled-up newspaper, tried to swat me, called me a mean little wretch. I am positive he thinks I am spoiled. He thinks I should go into the Scottish army or something, the way he did. I think he is a pain in the neck. He doesn't do much except read the racing form and lie around our house, if you ask me. I think he is a waiter at some restaurant. I pity the poor people who eat there.

Only once did I think the D.D. was interesting. That was one year when Mooch and Gac had a big Halloween party and everybody came in costumes and masks. The D.D. came as Mae West. You could have fooled me. I thought it was the real Mae West. "Got you that time, sonny," he laughed, striking out at me with his paw and purse. Why he always wanted to hit me, I don't know.

Once I overheard Gac say to Mooch, "I wish he would go back to Kilmarnock." But Mooch thought the D.D. was funny, and he often took the D.D. with him when he went out to play golf, the D.D. dressed these times in plus-fours and a cap, because, as he said, "We invented the game and that's the way she's played back home."

Today, when we arrived home from the beach, there was the foolish D.D. sitting on the front porch in his kilt and holding the gnarled walking stick he sometimes carried that I had to watch out for. He looked like some mournful dog, and no wonder. He told Gac that he had lost his job and could he come and stay with us "for a few wee months." She hesitated, looked at Mooch, and then said, "Bring your things over. Two months only." The D.D. looked relieved and so did everybody.

We all went in, showered, changed--the D.D. threw a ball at me he found in the hall--and then we heard Gac calling out, "Soup's on!" Again, great whoops of laughter.

"How's my Maud doing?" Dude boomed out in that big voice of his.

"I don't know what's happened. Maud's shrunk," said Gac.

Huge laughter from Dude, and now Ike joined in with that high laugh that spiraled up to heaven.

"Why is Maud so funny?" I asked Maggie.

"Maud has this habit of shrinking every time your mother cooks her," Maggie said. "She's supposed to be an English roast, but she always comes out looking like some poor benighted old beastie. It was Dude who christened her Maud."

That's the way we went into dinner, everybody laughing hysterically, thinking that Maud was the funniest thing in the world. And everybody made a toast to the D.D., wishing him luck in finding a new job, and the D.D. popped up and made a speech thanking everybody and giving Gac a quick kiss. You know what I think? I think Gac makes the best damn Maud in the whole world.

It's clear that Mooch agrees with me. He pops up now to propose a toast to the chef whom he calls "Maud's mother" and he promises to take us kids to the World's Fair on Saturday. But wouldn't you know the D.D. would have to go and spoil everything? The D.D. announces he is going with us and that he fully intends to wear the kilt in honor of the occasion. Who wants to go marching into the World of the Future with a crazy Scotsman? My mother whispers to me, "Forgive and forget." Well, I don't!

The World's Fair of 1939! Better than the circus, better than the beach, it was a streamlined rocket straight to the moon for us! We piled into the car, Mooch driving, Skeezix squeezed in between Mooch and the D.D. in the front seat. Gac, Laurie, and I rode in the back seat. I brought my Brownie camera with me to take pictures.

To begin with, we had to worry about the weather, because it had been overcast in the early morning, but the sun began breaking through, and by the time we got to Flushing Meadow, the sun was out, so we were happy.

What I worried about never happened. People didn't look at us as though we were peculiar, having the D.D. in his kilt walking with us. In fact, they seemed to smile and like his appearance. That was news to me.

We had to go to all the different pavilions of nations first. I remember Italy and the Soviet Union. I thought they were the most impressive. Gac had her eye on the French pavilion, said she wanted to have lunch there, but Mooch took one look at the prices and said, "Nothing doing." Laurie wanted to go to the General Motors pavilion, and we had to wait almost an hour and a half just to get in, but it was worth it. We sat on comfortable chairs that slid along and showed us the World of the Future. And I saw television for the first time and was actually on it, and so was the D.D. He did a little highland fling, and all the people who were standing around waiting their turn applauded him.

The thing I wanted most to do was to go on the parachute jump. Mooch had said yes, but Gac said no, and I made such a fuss that Laurie said I was spoiling everybody's day. Then, out of the blue, the D.D. said he wanted to go on the parachute jump, too, and he would take me with him. Well, you can just bet I started changing my mind about him and all Scotsmen right then and there. I jumped up and down in an over-enthusiastic manner so Gac wouldn't be able to turn me down. I was right. She didn't.

Of course it took almost another hour before the D.D. and I even got up to the entrance. While we were inching up in the line, the D.D. told me about a lot of his adventures. He was in the British army in World War I, where he had had mustard gas thrown at him in a trench, and it affected his hearing. I didn't know he had married a Frenchwoman and that they had had a daughter who had died of infantile paralysis. Then his wife went back to France, and he never heard from her again. Kind of a sad thing, I thought.

I can tell you I was plenty scared when we began being pulled up to the top of the parachute jump. You go up what looks like a long cable, and, then, when you hit the top, watch out! You drop like a shot, and the whole world looks like little ants among green velvet rows down below. Then you glide down nicely to a smooth landing, and that's it.

I thanked the D.D. for taking me, and he shook my hand. Gac snapped a photo of us standing at the exit from the parachute jump. The D.D. put his arm around my shoulder. The World's Fair of 1939 was the first time I realized that Scotsmen might be okay.

THE DAY AFTER THE EARTHQUAKE

The God's honest reason why I picked up this guy in the first place was that I was suddenly scared to death to find myself on the surface of the moon the day after the earthquake. You know how it is in California once you go inland from the coast. It's one hideous desert with clumps of green and brown communities miles apart, like Bakersfield, King City, Soledad, Paso Robles, and so on. Everyone driving from San Francisco to L.A. and vice versa hustles through these long dry patches to get to the green places on time. Well, there I was, tooling along on Highway 46, coming up from Route 5 in L.A., when the whole world suddenly turned dry and yellow, with the sun sitting so hot on me that I wouldn't have been surprised if all California busted into flames or I got swallowed up by a hundred aftershocks.

I mean, sure I'm a good kid and all, but it was my first long trip on the new bike, heading up to Salinas for the races. I thought I was losing my mind, seeing a mirage or something, when what I saw in the distance as a tall cactus turned out to be a human being hitchhiking in this God-forsaken landscape. I stopped without thinking. "Where you going?"

This big guy, about twice my age, kind of smiled as though he thought I was funny. "West, same way you're going." His tee-shirt said "INSTANT ASSHOLE. JUST FILL WITH ALCOHOL," but he looked okay to me and sounded decent.

"Hop on," I said. "Name's Jay."

"Pete," he said, strapping on his gear and swinging his leg up over the back like a man who knew bikes. "Let's go."

The minute we hit the pavement a crazy thought buzzed through my head about should I have picked this guy up. I was only twenty-four and didn't know everything.

A few minutes out, we saw one of them welcome California oases coming up--a combination gas station and restaurant--civilization.

"Pull in," Pete shouted, poking me in the ribs.

I pulled in to a little white ticky-tacky restaurant.

"Need some chow," said Pete. "How about you? I'll buy."

"Sure." Pretty nice guy, I thought. I rolled the bike around and parked it under a big tree with some plaques and a kind of a garden around it.

"'Under the spreading chestnut tree,'" said Pete, laughing. We went into the restaurant. Empty. But out from the kitchen popped a real cute blonde waitress who gave us a big Suzanne Somers smile and jiggled away with us following her like hounddogs to a table by the window.

"Father and son?" asked Suzanne.

"Nope," said Pete. "Gentlemen of the Road."

"I figured that," said Suzanne, throwing a couple of menus at us. "If you're James Dean fans, you came to the right place." I followed her eyes. They had lots of posters and photos on the walls. There he was in all his glory, James Dean, lounging against a tree, smiling like he knew some kind of secret. I looked at Pete. "My mother had that poster from when she was in high school," I said. "She won't throw it out."

"Is that so?" said Pete.

When Suzanne brought our orders, she leaned over real low to me and said in a soft voice, "You know, honey, you look an awful lot like him. You got those same hurt, innocent eyes." Pete hooted and shot out a jet of water from his mouth which set Suzanne to giggling. I stiffened up and said, "Yeah, well I ain't no dumb James Dean."

"Do you know," said Suzanne standing back a little, kind of addressing the two of us, "James Dean died in a car crash not six hundred yards from here?" Her eyes indicated the tree with my bike parked under it.

"Is that what that is?" I said.

She looked at Pete as though she were challenging him. She crossed her arms which pushed her boobs out more. "I bet you know all about James Dean, don't you, Daddy?"

"You bet I do," Pete replied, handing her his dirty plate.

"Jeez, I always got James Dean confused with Bob Dylan and Elvis," I said, kidding her, playing her game.

But Suzanne was zeroing in on Pete now. "You ready for some coffee now, honey?" she asked.

"Sure," Pete said, giving her a big cat-like smile and a yawning stretch that showed off his pumped-up biceps and the sweat stains on his tee-shirt. "You make me feel right at home here in Cholame. That's nice."

Suzanne hustled back and poured the coffee. "How'd you know this town's called Cholame?" she asked him.

"Yeah," I said. "How'd you know that, man?" "

"Sign out there says so," Pete replied. "I keep my eyes open at all times."

"You are in the heart of Cholame--post office, restaurant, James Dean Memorial, all in one," said Suzanne.

"But there's more to the story," said Pete.

"You are so right," said Suzanne, giving him the glad eye again.

"Jay here needs a little kindergarten lesson," said Pete.

"What are you talking about?" I said. I didn't like being taken for a fool.

Suzanne suddenly leaned down, putting her elbow on the table and resting her chin in the palm of her hand. She looked me straight in the eye in an embarrassing way. Her voice got real low. "Would you like a Coke or a Pepsi now?"

"Maybe a Coke," I said to get her out of my face. She headed for the counter and went out into the kitchen.

"Get her to tell you about James Dean," Pete whispered to me mysteriously.

"He don't interest me," I said, but Suzanne came back with the Coke, squeezed in next to me on the bench, planting her butt squarely next to mine as though we were old friends. I noticed she and Pete made a lot of eye contact and I figured they'd probably get something going between them.

"Jay, you are not going to believe what I am about to tell you," said Suzanne, pressing her thigh flat against mine.

"Time out," I said. "What's your name?" I figured she was crowding me this close, the least she owed me was her name.

"You can call me Hey You," she said, pursing her mouth into a sexy little pucker, holding me spellbound with those innocent blue eyes. Then when she let her swooping hand fall, she patted me a good one high up on my thigh, brushing my crotch. Pete roared his asshole head off. I felt my face flush red, so I straightened up. "We gotta go."

"I'm sorry," she said. "Oh, honey, I'm sorry. I ain't gonna harm you. I just want to give you the real James Dean story because you are here at this national monument and I am the official tour guide, the only one who can give you the truth. Do you know what I'm talking about?"

"He knows what you're getting at," said Pete.

"I asked him, not you," she snapped. "You just sit still. If you keep your ears open, you might learn a thing or two yourself."

"Yes, Ma'am," said Pete super-sarcastically, giving me a what-the-hell-can-you-do look, but I noticed she gave Pete a smile of triumph and a wink in return.

"I'll 'fess up," she said. " I was only joshing you 'cause you're just a sweet, young kid who wouldn't know James Dean from the head of your pecker, now, would you? You weren't even born in 1955."

"You got it."

"Guess how old I am?"

"Twenty-five?" I lied.

"I am thirty-one, Jay. My real name is Marlona. My mother lives right there in that house you could see if you went five miles down that road veers off to the left and looked in that little old ranch house. Now, you just listen to me, see? James Dean was driving his Porsche on the day he died, and he was driving up to the races in Salinas with his agent, and they did hit a car not six hundred yards from here, and crashed, and some nice Japanese man did build this monument to him around that tree out there in the parking lot. That part's all true. But, do you know where James Dean and his agent spent their last night alive the night before they crashed?"

I shook my head.

"They spent the night in my mother's house. Now, what do you and the *National Enquirer* think of that little bit of news? My mother knew who that young actor was. He was really wiped out, so she helped him into the shower and into bed, and he pulled my mother in with him . . . and . . . you are looking at the daughter of James Dean. I never collected a penny. I never wrote a book. Neither did my mother. We didn't figure to capitalize on any of it because my mother had real respect for him. I mean REAL RESPECT. She named me Marlona because she said James Dean idolized Marlon Brando and told her right in bed, even as they were doing it, that he wanted to give the world another Marlon Brando."

"Bullshit," shouted out Pete dramatically, slamming down his coffee mug on the table.

Marlona clutched me as though she was scared to death. She hooked her hand through my belt and threw her other arm across my chest as though we were acting out some Wild West show. "What do you mean?" she screamed at him. "You gonna let him say that to me, Jay?"

"Hold on," I said, but Marlona bolted up from the table, shoved me down in my seat, and ran behind the counter, stooping down low.

"Get out," she shouted like some psycho actress. "The two of you."

I wondered what in hell kind of madhouse she was running here that we had stumbled into.

"You get your ass over here and sit down," said Pete to her in this calm big cop's voice. "And bring that pot of coffee with you."

To my surprise, Marlona did as she was told. Her eyes were all obedience now, like a well-trained dog, as she watched Pete. She was still breathing hard, though, with a lot of rage inside her.

"Thank you, kindly," said Pete politely. "Now, both of you kids just sit down and listen up carefully." Marlona sat down next to me again, but a little apart, just in case he should say something that would make her spring up and attack.

"The reason I know you're lying," said Pete, "is that the real truth is known only by me. It is all in a book that is on the publisher's table right now in New York. That publisher's name, by the way, is Alfred Knopf, in case either of you wants to make a phone call. What you two don't know is that I was born in Fairmount, Indiana, in 1936, five years after my older brother. Our daddy left us and we were raised baseball-playing Quakers by an aunt and uncle. My brother wanted to be an actor, and so he went off to New York, did some television, some commercials, some porno, I think, and a play by a Frenchman named André Gide. My brother studied at the Actors' Studio with this director named Elia Kazan who brought him to Hollywood. Now, I was mechanically inclined, and so I worked on cars and bikes in South Bend, Gary, and, finally, Chicago. I decided two years ago that it was time I cashed in a few of my chips, so I have been writing the story of my brother from my point of view. I am out here putting on the finishing touches, you might say. I've been talking to Jane Withers and James Whitmore and now I'm heading up to the races to complete what my brother never did."

You could have knocked me over. As for Marlona, she didn't say nothing, just got up and went back into the kitchen. "Yeah," I said. "I want to look at that tree, but we better hit the road if we're gonna get there. We got to head over to Route 101 north. I want to wash up first."

"Right," said Pete. "Give me the keys and I'll start up the bike. I'll just pay Miss Marlona D. Light for her good service and her entertaining but lying story."

I tossed him the keys, got up and went into the restroom to wash up. Took my shirt off. Splashed water on my face and chest. Stuck my head under the tap. It felt real good. When I came out, Marlona was fiddling with the lock on the door. "Still here?" she said. "Thought you left with him."

"What do you mean?"

"He's gone. I thought you both left."

I looked out the door. My bike was gone. There was just a hazy swirl of dust around the tree where I had parked it. "Jesus Christ," I said. "He stole my bike." I felt for my wallet. "He got my wallet, too."

"Maybe you lost it," said Marlona. "Look, I'm sorry, but I'm locking up."

"That son of a bitch set me up," I said. "He took my four hundred bucks and my bike."

"Well, I can't help you, sonny," she said, practically pushing me out the door. "I got an important church meeting this evening."

"Big deal," I said. By now I was getting so paranoid I felt she must have been in on the whole con, too. I mean, why was she always rubbing up against me, like feeling me up, you know? I watched her drive off in a silver Nissan she had parked behind the store. I pictured her meeting Pete and my motorbike at a bar somewhere and then the two of them riding off to her house in town, rolling around in the bedsheets with my four hundred bucks clinging to their sticky bodies. I wrote down her license number just in case I wanted to do something about it, but what could I prove?

That big shady tree was the center of this oasis at Cholame. Around it was built a series of tablets, wood railings, and a stone garden. Some Japanese guy provided all that. He put his thoughts into words. I read what he wrote a couple of times. One tablet said that James Dean was just a young man who became an actor, appeared in a few plays and three movies. He was a sweet, sensitive person who had all the people of the 1950s identifying with him. The donor wrote that the tree was called the Tree of Heaven and that he had built this little memorial in honor of what the young man's life had meant to everyone. I thought that this Japanese man and that James Dean he talked about must have been two of the best people on earth, not like those shitheads Pete and Marlona.

In the middle of the memorial a plaque said that James Dean's favorite saying was "The essential is always invisible to the eye," which he read in a book called *The Little Prince* by some Frenchman. Why'd the man have to spoil it by putting up a crappy saying like that?

I decided to thumb my way back home then. I thought of Pete zapping around on my bike and me in his place hitchhiking to hell and back. I told myself to forget about the races. But after half an hour nobody had picked me up yet. Once in a while a car stopped out front, someone jumped out and ran over to read the plaques around the tree. A few people smiled at me, and one guy stared at me too long, I thought, as though he recognized me, but nobody said anything, so I said nothing, too. I was really pissed off at everybody, especially myself.

It made me so damn mad that just a few hours earlier I had had my bike and my four hundred bucks, and now I had nothing, not even a ride, not even a hope. I took out my pocket knife and tried to pry that James Dean plaque loose. He got me into this. I figured he owed me something. I hated all those teen-age idols, anyway, Elvis included. But the dumb plaque broke my knife point. Wouldn't you know?

The Last Major Appearance
of Baker Tompkins

The reason I'm standing here in front of the video camera telling you all this is that it's a rehearsal for what's to come. I'm trying to get my bearings right now since I just got safely through Penn Station and into my room in this what-a-dump hotel where I got a special rate of two nights for sixty bucks, so that's not too bad when you consider that this is where it all will end. About time, too, if you ask me. You can't do anything these days, even suicide, without paying through the nose.

Anyway, you could say I'm enjoying New York, even if I haven't seen much of it, only the Port of Authority Bus Terminal and the hellish subway that brought me down to 34th Street and Penn Station which I had to walk through. "Deliver me from Penn Station." I didn't think it was so bad, but people on the bus coming up from Virginia had warned me to hold on to my wallet with both hands, walk fast, and don't talk to anybody or stop even to buy a paper or a hotdog. Muggers were hanging from the streetlamps on every corner, they said. Well, nothing happened. Maybe it was the time of day.

I got the whole idea from a story we had to read in school. Would you believe it? The story was the only one I liked. It was called "Paul's Case" by some woman called Willa Cather. I liked her name immediately, even when the teacher first mispronounced it as Willa Catheter. It made me laugh. But the story made me think. I really understood the boy in that story. What happened is he came from that boring blot in Pennsylvania called Pittsburgh, sneaked away to become an usher at Carnegie Hall in exciting old New York, got grounded by his stupid father who didn't understand the first thing about life and art, stole some money, like who cares anyway, and ended up in a big splurge at the Waldorf before the idiots caught him, but he fooled them and opted for a neato suicide instead.

The whole town couldn't figure out why he did it. I knew instantly. Picardy, Virginia, isn't exactly the liveliest place on earth. I didn't exactly have slews of friends, being brought up as the only Christian Scientist in town with the dumb name of Baker Eddy Tompkins, thanks to my mom who behaved like a fanatic about our religion and dragged us all on one-hundred mile roundtrips to Richmond weekly because there was no Reading Room in Picardy, only Baptists and Whiskepalians. It didn't help either when my Dad died of pneumonia because, as everybody said, she refused to ship him off to the hospital at the right time, but instead had us all calling practitioners on the phone. Until then, I thought Science was harmless enough, but Dad's passing convinced me the whole thing was a crock, so here I am. I can just see Mom wringing her hands and saying, "That moonish, bookish boy, what's he up to?" But I know she'll put an optimistic spin on it as she always does, so I'm satisfied my ultimate demise won't faze her one bit.

"BAKER EDDY DONE IN AT SIXTEEN. LAST WORDS, 'TOO BAD, CRUEL, FUCKING WORLD!'" God, I wish they'd print that as the headline in the Picardy *Picayune-Express*.

Do you know what I'm planning to do tonight, just before the final message? I'm going to watch Mickey Rourke in *Wild Orchid*. I've never seen it. You can't get a hold of that video in the entire uncommonwealth of Virginia. I hear it's better than *Nine and a Half Weeks* which I did see. Boy, that Kim Basinger's something else. Mickey really made her look like a great actress, didn't he, and, of course, she's stunning and has that sensational body. I think Mickey Rourke is the best movie actor in the business. I believe everything he does. I can see right into his soul. He has these big, brown eyes like a dog's, that let you know everything he's thinking and feeling. I wish he were my brother or my father. If I had a pet of any kind I would name him Mickey, just in honor of Rourke. He comes from Miami, you know. For a while I considered going to Miami or to West Hollywood and trying to find him, just to ask him for some advice. I think he'd feed me a few answers. He's had two professional boxing matches, so he's tough and you can trust what he says. Have you ever seen his arms and his tattoos? Fantastic biceps. Great looking man, just the opposite from me, but that's why I figure I could learn from him. And when it comes to humping, Mickey's a champion high rider. None of my ex-friends back home likes him. They prefer Harrison Ford or Kevin Costner. God, what wimps!

Well, I almost went to Harvard once. Not quite, but Mickey played a Harvard dude in *Nine and a Half Weeks*. He wore this business suit and did the suave Wall Street thing by day and whipped Basinger into shape by night, and I think he had a law degree or something, so that temporarily inspired me, and I told everybody about it, making them think I had reformed or something, and I was in everybody's good graces for a while, but then they found out it all came from the movies, and, zippo, that was the end of the promise and the spotlight for me.

Mickey's will be the last flick I will ever see. Once, I wanted to be a filmmaker and make movies that would star him. He did one called *Homeboy*, which he liked, and so did I, and he did a wonderful film about Ireland and England called *A Prayer for the Dying* in which he was an I.R.A. rebel trying to blow up the whole Gibraltar-faced Maggie Thatcher world, like why should the English be lording it over the Irish the way they did over India? And he aced a little Charles Bukowski epic called *Barfly* with Faye Dunaway in which he smashed up every bartender he came into contact with. I thought that was pretty special, too. Who cares about bartenders anyway? What good do they do? They are fake psychiatrists who just feed people more booze. I've heard Mickey's got to watch out for that, too, in real life. Maybe that's why I've ironically settled on booze as a way of death. Maybe it's also why I'm here in New York. It could be the basic Martin Scorsese in me. I know it's not the Woody Allen. I don't intend to go anywhere near the Russian Tea Room and fall under its rosy spell, as Woody has. I'm not interested in pleasant futures and tranquil pasts anymore, Mia Farrow be damned.

How I arrived at this terminal state is that I followed the advice of our vocational counselor in school. We had to sit down and decide what I was going to do in life, he said, follow some plan or have some career objective in mind. He said my idea of just filming daily life in Picardy to make it into a documentary that would expose the hyopcrisy of its mores and social customs wouldn't wash. He said it would only end up by being as embarrassing as Michael Moore's epic on General Motors, *Roger and Me*, which he didn't think was very hot. He just laughed when I suggested I might eventually write something for Mickey. He didn't even know who he was. He was so out of touch he hadn't even seen *Diner*. He thought I should think along the line of computers, but I told him I hated DOS and Basic and always wondered what studying Finnish would be like, or how do you say "shit" in Swahili, or what would my name be in Gaelic, and he replied that I didn't have the right attitude, and, in fact, he didn't like the constant smirk on my face, which he interpreted as meaning I thought I was superior or something to everyone in Picardy, and when I replied, "Well, I am, especially to you and all the other slowmos in Pittsburgh," he said to get my ass out of his office, get a life and I'd better add up my pluses, if any, and my minuses to find out what kind of a miserable human being I was, and I did, and he's right--I am quite unsatisfactory.

Number one, there's not much upstairs, just a few things on the right side of the brain--I can draw a little, sing in a lyric tenor voice, Irish revolutionary tunes mostly, except when people are listening, and I can definitely say what's on my mind without shaking, but a lot of people think because I'm quiet, I'm smart, and I know that's not true. I really don't know much and I don't seem to want to know some things. I'm too selective, I suppose. I resisted all mathematics, for instance. I told every teacher I ever had that it was a philosophy I totally quarreled with and that I didn't care whether Pythagoras, Euclid, or some other damned Greek, or even a Chinese, had invented it, the whole thing was wrong and I opposed it. This was a major setback for my education, you can well imagine.

Second, I'm pretty puny to look at. Five feet, eight inches, one hundred thirty-four pounds. What's that? Nobody's attracted to me. Not even homos. My face is kind of thin and pale. Maribeth Loomis said I had a nice smile, so I asked her out to a dance last year, but that was a total disaster. She bopped me in the balls when she sat down, which I thought was an accident, but it wasn't, it was sexually intentional, and when she smiled and said, "I'm sorry, I didn't mean to surprise you," I replied indignantly, "Well, you did," which was the God's truth, but the wrong thing to say, so Richard Manalaro told me, he who knows everything about women. According to that oracle, I should have said, "Let the games begin" or, "Foreplay's over," something like that. You can easily see I'm a total failure at sex. Maribeth Loomis dumped me after that. I would see her and her friends giggling about me whenever I buzzed around, trying to act cool and make up. Once, a guy I hated said to me in the locker room, "What's the matter, don't you Christian Scientists fuck either?" Sex is worse than Antarctica for me. It's something I'd have to put on my list for Mickey to explain to me. He's a poet laureate in that department.

Third, Picardy public opinion is completely right, for once. I totally lack any career objective or direction in life. I just mope around a lot, waiting to be discovered, I suppose. My mom says I've seen too many motion pictures. "You're kidding," I say in mock horror, which is wasted on her. "Here in Picardy where they've shown *Mary Poppins* a zillion times and where *Beauty and the Beast* had to be held over a third week?" That's when I bought this video camera and started documenting life in Picardy. I thought it might convince people and me that I did, indeed, have some kind of focus on the future. But it didn't work. People kept saying I should begin by bagging groceries at the Safeway or slinging pizzas at the Pizza Hut, but I can't stand the Pizza Hut mentality and the Safeway manager just wouldn't hire me, for some reason.

So I took the four hundred samolians I had saved up for my indefinite future and decided to come here to New York for the quick squish, the final snuff. How I'm going to do it is most interesting and very filmic. I'm planning on buying two bottles of Booth's gin later this afternoon. It's 90-proof, the most powerful, I've been told. Then, I'm going to find out what it's like to get really drunk while I watch Mickey roll around with his girlfriend in *Wild Orchid*, and I figure by the final reel, I'll be blissfully bombed, having learned a few things, and then I'll turn on this video camera for my last major appearance with a final salute to Mom and a tribute to Mickey for the sweetness in his soul and a few words about take-this-town-and-shove-it to my beloved Picardy, with a little footnote of thanks to Willa Cather for her brilliant idea, and a business message to the hotel desk to return the *Wild Orchid* video, please, and to clean up the mess by just burning my skinny remains with no funeral or nothing, thank you, and they can give the maid any gin I might not have consumed, and I'm sorry to have caused anybody any trouble, and thanks to all for their noble efforts. That's about it. What more's left to say? Did you expect me to say goodbye to clocks ticking, mama's apple pie, the old town church clanging out the hour, and the old stage manager coming your way? Not me. Not Mickey Rourke's kid. It's a Maggie Thatcher special in your face, world. Th-th-th-that's all, folks!

Love,

Baker Eddy M. Rourke Tompkins

FINDING MICKEY ROURKE

After my stupid botched-up suicide attempt, which I'm truly sorry you didn't read about in the Noo Yawk *Daily Noose*, *National Enquirer* or the Picardy, Virginia, *Times-Picayune*, I was thrown out of that crummy Manhattan hotel by the Assistant Manager and the maid. God, it made me retch that much more. For all my dramatic effort, I didn't even rate the manager. Hell, I stayed there only because Mickey Rourke had lived in that dump back in the 80s. But what do they know--bunch of welfare recipients and drug addicts. I honored them by attempting the fatal squish there and filming it on my video camera. So, it didn't turn out and I hurled up that potent Booth's 90-proof gin all over the place and passed out. Did they have to toss me out like that? Even though I'm only sixteen and didn't grab the sensational headlines I'd hoped for, isn't the mere attempt worth some applause? The damn fools in that place didn't even remember Mickey. Fat lot of sense that dumb Hotel Earle makes.

Well, naturally I had to burn all my suicide notes--the one to my mother, the great Christian Scientist in Picardy, whose five thou is financing this whole odyssey; the one to Mickey, my main man; and the one to Willa Cather who gave me the whole idea in the first place via her story "Paul's Case." Yes, I know she's passed over, but you know we Christian Scientists don't really acknowledge death. We think all people are on some sort of permanent spiritual tether so that you can get in touch with them whenever you really set your mind to it.

Now that I had no place and no destination anymore, I had to revamp my plans. I decided to head for Hollywood and go straight to the source--Mickey Rourke. He would have to take me in, sit me down, give me some solid advice. I mean, Jesus, I was like his kid brother, wasn't I?--spiritually, of course, not literally. So I took the Greyhound bus to Chicago, but that took fifteen hours, and I found it more expensive than it should be, so I got a last-minute cheapo flight out of O'Hare to Los Angeles and went straight to Red Ruby Productions, Mickey's company, on Santa Monica Boulevard in the heart of ticky-tacky Hollywood. I just waltzed right in, pushed the door open into a huge room painted black with cardboard movie mock-ups of tough-guy Mickey with overcoat and fedora hat on, Mickey as boxer, numerous photos of him in different flicks, and a wrap-around desk-counter, behind which a young woman stood.

"Yo," I said, "Is Philip André around?"

"Who are you?" she said. "What do you want?"

"The name's Tompkins," I replied. "I'm a writer. Got an idea for development with Mickey. Where's the man?"

"Not here," she said, kind of pushing me toward the door. "I'll give him the message. Give me your card."

"Not necessary," I said. "I don't deal cards. Look, I gotta talk with him."

"He's not here," she said. "He's in Florida."

"Oh, really," I said, disbelieving her. "I'll be back."

"Tompkins?" she said. "I'll tell him you stopped by."

"Thanks," I said, looking around. "Nice place. Got a boxing ring here, I understand."

"Yes. Upstairs. Well, thanks for coming." And she closed the door on me. I went down the stairs and out the door. A beat-up car with Florida plates was parked in front of the building. "Well, what do you know?" I said.

Out on my ass on Santa Monica Boulevard. But not for long. I put two and two together. Mickey's a Florida guy, get it?, and we got a car here with Dade County, Florida plates on it. Guess what? The back door to the car is unlocked on the street side. So I eased around before I planned anything out and slid in, scrunching way down on the floor, close to the two front seats. Wow, I thought, you're shaking all over. Calm down. You want to see your idol, don't you? Well, he's gonna be driving this heap with you in it somewhere soon--probably Rodeo Drive in Beverly Hills and then you can pop up and say hello, thanks for the ride to Armani's and all. And then Mickey will probably want to treat you to lunch at the Ivy or Morton's and we'll cruise the babes on Sunset and polish off a few brews and pizzas at Spago before making our way up Benedict Canyon past Heidi Fleiss' house and Jay Leno's until we come to the cabin Mickey was building until he lost it, but we'll crash there anyway--squatters' rights, no autographs, please, we're not signing today, and no photographs, except for *Paris Match*. They can take all they want--*Les Amis de Mickey Rourke*.

Well, that's the way it should have happened and would have if it were a Preston Sturges' flick, but what actually turned up was some dude with long hair opened the front door, spotted me right away, said "Get the fuck out of there, creep," threw me out on the sidewalk and drove off without another word, as though he were used to finding creeps in his car all the time. Well, hell, this is Hollywood, I thought. What do I know? Creeps on every corner, I guess, including me. So I picked myself up, took a local bus to downtown L.A., grabbed a hamburger and a coke at Wendy's, and then took another bus out to LAX where I got standby on a flight to Dallas-Ft. Worth, and from there a direct flight to Miami, where I got another bus to South Beach.

Jesus, more palm trees, I thought. Stinking pink Art Deco hotels, bars, and apartment houses, right off the back lot at Twentieth-Century. Now I understood where Mickey got all that experience punching out drunks and bartenders and why he was so perfect in the Bukowski epic *Barfly*. He and Dunaway must have had a blast. Maybe they trained here, even though *Barfly* was probably meant to be some shit hole like California's Venice where the sun never sets because it doesn't bother rising in the morning.

"Hey, man," I said to the first guy I saw walking on Ocean Boulevard. "Where's Mickey Rourke's in-your-face bar?"

"Sorry," he said. "I gotta run."

What the hell, what's the rush? I thought. So I saw another man trying to clean off dog shit from his shoe, almost falling over from the effort to hop on one leg. "Don't bother me, asshole," he said. "Can't you see I got a problem?"

A taxi driver eased into the curb, dropped off a blonde woman totally dressed in black, who smiled at me, and then went into a little purple and orange hotel. I zapped around to talk to the driver. "You know where Mickey Rourke's in-your-face bar is?" I asked.

"Mickey Rourke?" said the driver. "Saw him on Letterman the other night. Had a little dog with him. Cute spot. Nah, his bar closed, kid. Don't know what happened."

"He's not here then?"

"Oh, he's a Miami man, all right. He goes up to Ft. Lauderdale, has a couple of prize fights, gets beaten up regularly by those black guys, keeps coming back. He's got guts, I'll say that for him. But he's messed up. Don't know what's happened to him."

"He's a great actor," I said hotly.

"Don't get me wrong," said the driver. "Yeah, he's a fine actor, but he's throwing it all away. Don't know what happened with the bar. Used to be down there around 10th and Ocean. Why don't you go there? That's where all the action is."

"Thanks," I said, starting to head back to the sidewalk.

"But, kid," he called after me. "Not at two-thirty in the afternoon. After ten at night." He touched his fingers to his cap lightly in a kind of salute and drove off.

The Traviata Hotel is a black and silver hotel with glass brick windows on the ground floor and it looks very smart and prosperous. It's right across from where Mickey's bar was, now closed, until a new tenant takes over. I wandered in, found a friendly red-haired woman behind the registration desk. "May I help you?" she asked.

"Well, yeah, I was wondering about Mickey Rourke's bar..." I said.

She sighed. "You and everybody else. He closed it."

"He's not here in Miama Beach?"

"Haven't seen him in months. He's an actor, you know. He's not just a boxer."

"I know that."

She sensed my annoyance. "Sorry. Some don't, you know. Around here, he's known as a boxer."

"What happened?" I asked.

"Didn't you read about it? It was in the papers, on television. He checked some kids' i.d.'s and they were underaged, so he threw them out. They hit at him, so he hit back. The police came and hauled him off. I don't know how it turned out. I guess the judge threw out the case, or something. Anyway, the bar was closed soon after that."

"Oh."

"What's your interest in all this?" she asked.

Before I knew what I was doing, I heard myself say: "Nothing, really. I'm just his brother, that's all."

"You're his brother? God," she said.

"Joey," I lied. "Been out of touch lately. Been to South America on a ship."

"Well, why don't you just ask your family about him since you live here?" she challenged. "Come on, you're not his brother. You're lying."

I turned and walked out. Why should I give her the time of day? She seemed to think it impossible that I could be related. To hell with her.

I found an age-disadvantaged guy sitting on a bench throwing out popcorn to a flock of pigeons. "They like that stuff," I said. "I'm Mickey Rourke's brother, Joey," I dropped casually.

"Yeah," the old man said. "I'm his grandfather, Isaac."

"No. I mean it," I said.

"Go to school, Joey," the old man said. "The bell's ringing. Don't deal drugs. Don't hassle old people. It isn't nice. We don't like it."

I walked away, went down toward the ocean, watched the waves breaking gently, felt the warm breezes coursing through the palm trees. Wondered if Spain and France were as hostile as Miami. Wished I could swim away. Knew France was better. They love Mickey. What good sense and taste the French have.

Along the beachfront, I saw a green and white awning over a cool white building and a sign reading *Havana Bar.*

"*Buenos tardes,*" I said to the bartender. "*Donde esta Mickey Rourke?*"

"*Mickey Rourke?*" he said, drawing his eyebrows together and kind of smirking at me. "*Non esta aqui.*"

I turned to leave.

"*Por que?*" he called out after me.

"*Non hay de que,*" I said.

I heard him laughing at me. Nobody understands.

I spotted a beautiful girl in a bikini lounging on the beach in glorious isolation, her body covered with suntan oil, and her long, dark hair spilling over her face and sunglasses. She sat up at attention when I approached. "What do you want?"

"I just wanted to ask you something?"

"I've got mace," she said. "Stop where you are. I've got a whistle. There's a police stand over there." She pointed toward the street.

"I'm trying to find Mickey Rourke," I said. "I was just at his former bar."

"Oh, get lost, will you?" she said, brushing sand at me.

"Do you know where he is?" I asked, retreating.

"He's a movie actor," she said. "For Chrissakes, he's in Hollywood."

"Thanks," I said, "for nothing."

She held up her whistle. "One, two, three . . . ." I reached the pavement now and walked fast out of that scene.

I found a newsstand and cruised the mags. Found one called *Entertainment* that clued me in to Mickey's being in New York making a film called *Bullet*. The mag called it a "low budget film," said the film was being shot on location in Brooklyn. It didn't say when, but the mag was brand new. I had to recoup my thoughts. But, first, I came back at ten-thirty that night. I must have ploughed through thousands of people searching for Mickey's face, but no luck. I decided the mag must be right.

Next stop, Brooklyn.

The trail led to the Plaza Hotel on Fifth Avenue in Manhattan. The clerk was horrified. "Mickey Rourke?" he said. "Dear God, no. He's not here anymore. Try the Ritz-Carlton." Same story. They said he checked out, moved into an apartment, they wouldn't say where. "We can't divulge that information," the desk clerk sniffed.

So I went to Nello's, a restaurant where I knew Mickey always hung out in New York. A waiter just arriving for work was helpful. "Listen, he's not in Brooklyn. He was in here last night. I can tell you where he's going to be this morning at 10:30. Do you know Bryant Park, down by the library, Fifth at 42nd? Well, that's where. You really his brother?"

"Yeah, thanks, Gotta go," I said, since I had only five minutes to get there and the Lexington Avenue subway was a few blocks away

Bryant Park. They had a big tent set up. Some big fashion show do. Ralph Lauren, many models sashaying around, bored looking people in the audience, too much makeup, lots of perfume in the air, photographers all over the place. You couldn't get in without some kind of pass. Lots of limos, taxis, and cars pulling up, causing a general slow-up. A grey stretch limo pulls up and suddenly I see Mickey Rourke himself piling out of the car. The crowd notices. They shout things at him, some not so nice. "Mickey," I call out. "Hey, Mickey, it's me. I found you."

"Fuck you," Mickey spits out, giving me the finger, but it wasn't meant for me, I don't think. I hope he meant the guy behind me who looked mean and angry when I turned around.

A dark cloud came over Mickey's face, but the two bodyguards with him pushed their way through the crowd and Mickey came so close that he brushed me as he passed and I almost fainted, but said in a very faraway voice, "Hello, Mickey." He didn't say anything, but patted me lightly on the head and gave me that famous Irish priest of a smile you see in his flicks sometimes that makes you want to become a Catholic on the spot. "God bless you, Mickey," I called out after him, but he had already disappeared into the tent where I guess Carré Otis, Claudia Schiffer, Vendela, and all those beautiful Lagerfeld and Gaultier people were waiting to welcome him.

Just seeing him was a real high for me. I felt so good marching up Fifth Avenue after that. I actually went into St. Patrick's Cathedral and lit a candle for St. Mickey of Rourke. I gave up being a Christian Scientist forever at that point.

Then, afterward, I went over and ordered a drink at the Waldorf-Astoria and toasted Willa Cather, Paul, and St. Mickey.

Tonight I'm planning on splurging at Nello's, and perhaps a certain friend will drop in with a couple of luscious models on his arm and I'll be invited over, naturally, and we'll chat about *film noir*, and *haute couture*, and about the fleetingness of fame, and, indeed, of all life, like the worldly sophisticates that we are.

Then, maybe, in a few days, I'll make a phone call. "Hello, Mom? Yeah, it's me. I'm coming home. Had my fill. I turned down their offer. By the way, Mickey sends his best."

THE STRUCTURE

On a sunny Wednesday in April a university student sits on a green metal bench in front of the architecture building waiting for a bus. His name is Davey Raiford Sanborn. He is a white male Caucasian, age twenty-six, five feet eleven inches tall, one hundred sixty-two pounds, blue eyes, brown hair, mesomorph. On his knees he is very carefully balancing the structure, aware that the annoying California wind is whipping through its open spaces. He turns it delicately so that the wind will pass through head on, rather than at an angle which endangers the balance of the whole thing.

It is a light, yet strong structure. He has worked on it a total of thirty-three hours--until five in the morning today to complete it. He has glued all the pieces together with epoxy and covered them with foil, carefully wrapped, so that each cube in the structure gives the appearance of being constructed of aluminum--fragile, yet boasting a certain tensile strength.

Each cube surrounds open space. That was his plan. There are two sections to the structure--one consisting of fifty cubes, and the other, attached to it about mid-section, consisting of forty cubes. Davey carries it gingerly, as though it is a large bird cage. He has discovered that he has to hold it away from his hips and knees when he walks and grip it firmly because of the rush of wind. He wishes the wind would stop. He hadn't counted on its being so breezy today.

Davey sees the bus approaching in the heavy noon-hour traffic on the Via Triumphans. He stands up, anticipating the extra wind currents the arrival of the bus will stir up. He stands back a little from the door, until the driver opens it. Then he carefully climbs into the bus, one hand dropping his token into the fare box and the other trailing behind him, carrying the structure like a waiter with a floating island on a dessert tray.

A quick glance shows him that the only available seats are on the side in the front or way in the back. He will not be able to make it down the aisle without bumping the structure into someone, so he sits down in the front and once again deftly balances the structure on his knees. He notices that other passengers are looking at the structure, wondering what it is, trying to guess its function, attempting to connect him to it and to themselves. He supposes somebody will speak in a minute and ask him all about it. He knows he can answer easily. He is full of information. He looks expectantly into several promising faces, but nobody speaks to him or asks him anything, and the old stone-faced man of a driver just keeps relentlessly pushing the bus down the road toward the center of town without so much as another glance at Davey or the structure

Davey keeps his eye on the structure now that he realizes he has failed with the passengers. It will not do to let his mind or eye wander too much. The structure could be damaged irreversibly. He appraises it critically, turning it slightly on his knees so that he can view it from the best possible angle, the way he intended it to be seen. His eye goes immediately to that critical joint in the third cube, the one he had so much trouble with. Has he patched it up properly? Will it hold? Why does one joint have to give him so much trouble? Has he really done the best work he can do on this project?

He decides that he hasn't. He knows all the weak points of his work. They don't really have to be pointed out to him. He didn't need the pontifications of Professor Grunewald. He didn't need the gratuitous comments, designed to buoy him up, from his fellow students. Maybe he isn't cut out for this at all. He sags a little, but feels the structure shifting weight onto his right knee, and so he straightens up again and holds the structure smartly to avert any kind of accident happening to it. He lets his breath out subtly, surrounding the structure with its warm influence, calling the structure by his secret name for it, *animus.*

It is his original work. He alone is responsible for it. It is an extension of his own mind and heart. He felt, even in the early conceptual stages of work, that this structure was somehow what he was destined to build. He put into it all his knowledge and experience. He created it out of daring and insolence, and, when he finished, he experienced that mixture of pride and uncertainty that all creators feel. But he also realized that what he felt didn't matter, after all. The marketplace is where all ideas, all projects, are ultimately judged. Such is the nature of art and of the merchants of art. If the structure expresses something important or novel to the world at this moment, then Davey wins. If it doesn't, he fails.

He reaches up now to pull the cord for his stop, and, suddenly, he feels the structure sliding perilously across his knees. A woman sitting across the aisle from him looks startled and involuntarily puts out her hand to catch the structure, should it fall toward the aisle. Davey recovers and slides the structure back to a safe position across his knees. He arcs his body over it now. He smiles at the woman to thank her. She does not return the smile, but abruptly looks out the window, as though annoyed with him.

The bus pulls to his stop. He waits until it is motionless, and then he leaves quickly and quietly. The bus pulls away in a hurry while he is still standing on the curb very close to the body of the bus. The rush of wind in the wake of the bus nearly blows the structure out of his arms and into the air. But he holds on and walks the two blocks to the two-room apartment in the old wooden house in which he lives.

Davey puts down the structure temporarily on the front porch. He fumbles in his pocket for his keys, finds the right one, opens the door, pilots the structure in and berths it on the living room couch in a soft, firm harbor where nobody can threaten or damage it in any way. Then he goes into the kitchen, takes a drink of water, re-enters the living room, and sorts through the mail lying on the floor below the mail slot. He looks at the telephone expectantly. But it doesn't ring.

He goes into his bedroom where he takes a long look at himself in the shaving-stand mirror on top of his bureau. He sees through the mask of the tired, haunted student into the eyes of the flawed creator of another failure. Then, very carefully, almost expertly, still looking at himself in the mirror, he reaches his hand into the top left-hand drawer of the bureau, pulls out the waiting revolver and puts a bullet through his head.

THE PROMOTION COMMITTEE

Here they come, the halt, the lame, and the blind. In their hands rest several people's futures. All are Ph.Ds, having written unreadable footnoted theses on the head of a pin for which some universities have draped them in mediaeval garb and pronounced them superior to lesser people with ordinary brains and maybe no degrees. Somehow we have all been chosen to serve on the promotion committee at this dump where we all teach. A dean or president probably made the appointments. "Mediocrity rises"--that's our motto here.

Hester leads the pack. Straight from the ladies' room to the coffee and doughnuts table. Just back from a Club Med vacation in the Caribbean with a tan that makes her look like a choice piece of horse leather, Hester is stuffing her face with food and drink once again. I gather the Club Med safari this time didn't turn up any real prospects for husband number two. Hester does this every year. Nothing substantial ever comes of it. Hester will go back to teaching French with that enormous gusto Wellesley gave her.

Pierre qualifies on two counts. He is both lame and blind. He is an historian out of the California system, known for his prodigious memory and his rotten treatment of wife number one. He gulled a student into becoming a slave for him, and, in return, married her after dumping wife number one who fled back to Los Angeles and Scientology. Pierre slumps into a comfortable chair in a corner, adjusts his sunglasses and rests his white cane across his aching legs. He isn't talking at the moment which is a blessing. Probably saving up his comments which he will deliver from Olympus shortly. Trained by Jesuits, Pierre comes on like thundering Jeremiah.

Serena is blocking the doorway and the sun behind it. She is a big, lumpish Gibraltar. She is dressed in her usual costume--combat boots, army fatigues, and a camouflage jacket. Serena apparently is on a permanent bivouac somewhere in life. At the moment she has Alex trapped and is hitting him with big-gun English Lit thunder. Could be she thinks literature is a heavy metal branch of computer science. Alex is in Math. He is boyish and is looking very shy and embarrassed as though he has a feeling Serena is trying to seduce him. She isn't. She only wants to inhabit him.

That leaves old Roland, turkey neck, turtle head, also in English Lit, but exuding that patronizing manner some Charlottesville people have--gabbing about The Lawn and Jefferson and The Episcopal Church as though it is all so reasonable, so genteel, so correct in every way. Roland is one of those oafish Anglophiles who runs over to Merrie Olde whenever he can. He has a turtle wife and five little tadpoles bearing prissy English names like Sarah, Andrew, Philip, Edward, and Elizabeth. Roland is the chairperson of the promotion committee. All Episcopalians automatically pass go and collect two hundred smackerolas in his estimation.

I am in Biology, which is why I can cast a jaundiced eye on the whole lot. I am a dissector by profession. Why people willingly submit to a system that says do this, do that, is beyond me, but what can you expect of a race of Ph.Ds? They are supposed to be teachers, but some can't communicate anything at all. Several can't complete a simple sentence. Serena, for instance, jabbers on like some demented Shelley Winters. And Alex, to my knowledge, has never read a book in his life. He didn't even know who the president of the United States was the last time I talked with him socially. No point in trying to converse with him. He only talks Math and Computerese. He told me his computer was more important to him than his wife. *Chacun*, say I.

We have been at it all morning. Five candidates for two promotion slots. That's the way this dump works. Quota systems for everything. Only two lucky people will be promoted. The Dean and the President will rubber-stamp the decision of this magnificent committee

Let's see. While the break is still on, let's recapitulate. Whom have we seen? Whom have we rendered judgment upon? I take that back: Upon whom have we rendered judgement (British spelling). Blimey, it's smashing being English. You can make multi points with Roland and Serena that way.

Four little sheep have been led into the slaughter house. Each has had to come in, sit at a table, answer questions and p. r. him or herself. Best hype wins the prize. The funniest one was Jamie, the artist. What an innocent. Jamie has only an M.F.A., is a kind of Tom Selleck guy, really laid back, very Hawaiian and Southern Californian, which is where he is from. Jamie regards himself as a latter-day Buddhist. He simply refused to compete. He brought no letters of recommendation, only an ill-put-together scrapbook of clippings about his art exhibits. Poor Jamie seemed genuinely hurt when old Roland told him he had to re-submit next year and play the game properly. Roland said someone would help Jamie get his stuff together. Looks like Jamie will remain an assistant professor for another year until he completes Sandpile I.

Donna Stoller, energetic, aggressive, set them all on edge. Her field is Education, a major strike against her. These Ph.Ds don't believe anyone who has ever taken even one Education course can possibly teach. Donna is an originator of plans, an idea person, and a follow-through type. The committee tried to hold her up for another year, also, like Jamie, claiming her Doctor of Education degree wasn't good enough, but Donna rumbled threats of grievances and law suits and stormed out of the meeting.

"Well," huffed Hester. "You can see what she's all about."

"I admire her," I said. Heads swiveled. If looks could kill . . .

"Yes, well . . . , " covered Roland. "Let's go on to the next candidate."

David Russwurm from Psychology was next.

"They're all nuts in Psychology," hissed Hester as David walked in the door, exuding confidence.

"What do you want to know?" smiled David.

An imperceptible intake of air from Roland who decided to go for humor. "Well, everything, I suppose."

"Okay. I was born in a trailer in Yellowstone Park."

"Mr. Russwurm," intoned Pierre. "What makes you think you should be promoted to full professor?"

There followed a rather charming duet between Pierre and David. "I'm so talented. I was educated in New York. I could make more money in clinical psychology. I am doing this dump a favor. I have garnered over seven hundred thousand smackolas in grant money."

Pierre: "But I have heard . . . . How do you answer that? . . . How can you be so positive? . . . What committee service have you rendered? . . . Why, then, did you leave NYU?"

David won. Only Pierre voted against him. There was an unsubtle undercurrent in Pierre's dissent, I'm afraid.

"I still think they are all mad," Hester whispered to me. "But David was right on top of everything."

Next up was Maggie St. John, a beautiful, self-assured Bryn Mawr graduate currently sleeping with the head of the anthropology department at a prestigious nearby university. Maggie knew all the answers. She was the quintessence of correct preppiedom, even had a degree from Oxford. Talked in the standard constipated south-of-England accent. Instant promotion to full professor. S-C-O-R-E!

One left to go. Sammy Madison, Georgian, chairman--May God forgive me, chair--of the History Department and thus technically Pierre's superior. Pierre ruled himself out on this one. Sammy was defensive and evasive, talking about his latest book on American history, giving the impression that because he was chair of the department he was above this inquisitorial type of star-chamber investigation and ought not to be talked to at all. I remembered that Sammy was a good friend of the ex-president of this dump. They were good old boys. Roland was all coffee and sympathy toward him. Sammy was Episcopalian and had two advanced degrees from the University of Virginia. Hester, Serena, and Alex said wait another year. Sammy had only been here three years. Roland and I voted in favor of his promotion. Pierre abstained. Sammy lost. I imagine he will look for another job--he's young enough--or contact the ex-president and send out a swat team after a few hides. I love seeing a little hell raised around here.

"Thank God, that's over," Serena trumpeted. "Let's go get some drinks."

"I need one," said Hester. "Coming?"

"I've got a fifty-mile drive," I answered.

"You, Roland, Pierre?" she insisted.

"Choir," said Roland.

"Oh, yes, it is Wednesday night, isn't it?" said Hester. Hester was a Quaker. I don't think they sing ever, Wednesday nights or any other.

"Sounds good," smiled Pierre. "Give me a hand here." So out he went, tapping his cane in front of him with Hester in all her tanned glory on his arm.

"Good night," I said to Roland.

"Thank you, thank you all," shouted out Roland. "I think you all put in a good day's work."

Outside, the sunset was burning far behind the tall dark trees. The dump's tower was clanging out the hour. The Promotion Committee's crack team spilled out into the twilight, heading home from the exalted halls of higher education once more, confident that their work today would at the very least look good in writing on the good old *curriculum vitae*.

ZEKE ON RATS
AND AGGRESSION

At the moment there is nobody I hate more than the Director of Student Housing. This person has got to be the stupidest, most insensitive, sadistic person in my life at this particular time, and that's saying a lot because quite a few of my friends are into pain and pleasure before dinner; they think it's sexy, or something.

I mean, why I should have to put up with this person called Zeke Blue is beyond me, especially since exclusive Lady Britomart College prides itself so much on having all incoming freshpersons fill out a form that asks you a lot of personal questions and then purportedly matches you up with someone you're supposed to be compatible with. Zeke with me? That's a real hoot now. That's like matching Michael Jackson up with Axl Rose.

The first words I heard out of him were libelous. He took one look at me and said, "Jackamundo, it's the Queen of Spades. To whom am I indebted for this shuffle?"

And I said, trying to be nice, "The Director of Student Housing, sweetie, so just put it all together and it spells you and me."

I could feel his hateful eyes etching into me. I mean, his scorn was so heavy it spattered. "You wear dresses yet?" he sneered, "and earrings in both ears?"

"This is just a little number I whipped up in Santa Monica," I said, giving him my innocent Diana Ross look. "Don't you like it?"

"Santa Monica?" he replied. "That's in Iowa, isn't it?"

I mean, why should I have to put up with this kind of East Coast insolence? First, he insults my race, then he insults my sex, and now he brings in my hometown. I hardly expected Lady Brit, well-known to be the poshest college in Connecticut, to be like this. I thought people would be friendly here, but, as luck and the Director of Student Housing would have it, I had to draw Rasputin Junior for my roommate.

I wouldn't mind too much if Zeke Blue were at all attractive in any way, or even interesting. But there's just no appeal there. He's simply a clone. Feature this: He's about five feet ten, a Bon Jovi dirty blond mane with an Axl Rose sweatband, bluejeans, boots, drives a Harley-Davidson bike, and lives with his family on Park Avenue. Can you believe it? In California we always looked up to Park Avenue. We thought it was fashionable. Somebody warned me that the whole East Coast had deteriorated, but I wouldn't believe it. Like a fool, I had to see it for myself and live with the decline-and-fall of it all as my roommate, no less!

Probably I shouldn't complain. I am at Lady Brit on a California scholarship set up by the Bel Air Lady Brit alumni for a person of African descent with talent. That's me. They were really sweet, the people who interviewed me, loved my style and all, said I was most courageous since I was a male person. They were heavily impressed with my dossier and all the gorgeous clothes I had made. They said such a person deserved the best possible advantages in education, and so here I am. But the Director of Student Housing refuses to divorce Zeke and me. Not till the end of the year, he says. God, it seems like eternity!

The only friendly overture Zeke ever made to me was when he said his parents were dying to meet me and would I come into the city and have dinner with them one night. Of course I said yes. I thought, this will be an experience, a real apartment on Park Avenue. I'll be able to see what it's like for myself rather than take Paramount's word for it. So he told me to come in and aim for the Carlyle Hotel and I would be right in his neighborhood, but what I discovered is that the subway doesn't go to the Carlyle or anywhere near it, so I had to pay a cabdriver ten dollars to drive me up from Grand Central and listen to this insane cabbie chatter on about the New York Mets or Jets or whatever it is, and he kept calling me "Miss" all the way. It was really too chilling, but finally I got there and I called Zeke's apartment, and he answered, and I said: "Well, I'm here at the Carlyle. What's next?"

"Amandine," he said. "Blast right over here. Two blocks down, hang a left, come in the side entrance. Fourth floor." Zeke always says "amandine" whenever he answers the phone. Apparently, it means "Ready, right away, or here, speaking," as in this case. Zeke tells me it's newspeak. I wouldn't know. I'm strictly from Iowa, as Zeke always reminds me.

I don't know what I expected of Park Avenue, but I do know what I found, and I must say it was quite a shock. Zeke's mother and father don't have a car. They ride these little fold-up bicycles everywhere. She is a female Zeke, has shaved her head totally bald like Sinead O'Connor, but wears different wigs to suit her moods. When she's feeling honest, you get the bald eagle itself, and that's the way she greeted me. She went to Lady Brit, too, is their leading Manhattan alumna, and obviously gives heaps of money to them all the time. That explains the presence of you-know-who-there. I'm sure he couldn't get in on native intelligence, the way the rest of us did.

The father is in real estate. He owns a third of western Connecticut, so he says. He is oozing over into New York state now, he tells me, conquering White Plains, Mount Vernon, Yonkers, and something called the Bronx. I think Zeke said his father owned the Bronx. I don't even know where it is, someplace south of Greenwich, I think. Zeke said

I pass through it when I come into New York. It can't be much. I mean, it isn't the Village, it isn't Midtown, it isn't Wall Street, it isn't Bloomingdales. So what else is there?

Somebody has been collecting paintings in the Blue household. They do have the most attractive paintings, I'll say that for them. It's not everybody who has original Kandinskys, Rothkos, Jackson Pollocks, and Julian Schnabels in their living room.

Zeke and his sister, Daphne, who also went to Lady Brit, sleep in coffins instead of beds. The mother showed me these and said she bought them for the kids because they looked so comfortable and she thought Zeke and Daphne ought to start getting used to them since they were going to end up in them. They look like wooden cocoons, but the mother had them lined with mink and had special stands built for them. Zeke's coffin-bed is polished mahogany while Daphne has burled walnut. She is married and lives in Rio de Janeiro. Her husband is in hotels. The mother said Daphne would love me, whatever that may mean!

They had some neighbors in for cocktails, although I believe it was really to show me off to them. One of the guests is the regular pianist at the Carlyle. He played a few songs for us on the Steinway, and I couldn't believe that he actually knew my favorite of all times, Noel Coward's "Mad about the Boy." He knew all the lyrics, too. What a sweet, dear man. And he came to cocktails with Gloria Vanderbilt, of all people. She's quite stylish, but older than I thought, and I made the most awful *faux pas* when I said I loved her jeans, but not on Brooke Shields. She said, rather icily, I thought, "You're thinking of Calvin Klein." And then I realized what I had said. But, later, she said she loved the outfit I was wearing. It was that black-and-yellow *blouson* shirt over black leather pants. I swiped the shirt idea from Pierre Balmain, but nobody ever notices, so I don't mention it. The pianist had to rush through drinks to get back to the Carlyle, so he played only three numbers, including mine, gave Lolly (That's Zeke's mother) a kiss, and away he and Gloria flew.

Oh, yes, another person I just loved at their place was Hannah Blue, Zeke's grandmother. She is just gorgeous. Ninety years old with a huge head of bright red Lucille Ball hair, and diamonds and rubies that would knock your eyes right out. She tells priceless stories and chug-a-lugs her whisky neat in a shot glass like John Wayne. She told me she rode a motorcycle in New York until she was eighty years old. She said it's the only reliable way to get around. I told her about this idiot cab driver who dumped me out at the Carlyle, and she verified he overcharged me and reached into her purse to give me ten greenies out of her own money. I think she was a little confused, though. She kept calling me "Angelina." How do you get "Angelina" out of "Robert?"

I have learned so much since I came here to Lady Brit. I mean, I have learned so much about human nature that I may just have to write a book. Well, it would be mostly about Zeke, so I guess it would be a book about inhuman nature. It would certainly hit the top of the lists. What I know about Zeke Blue, what I have seen, what I could tell about him and his sordid affairs would make Jackie Collins want to inhabit him immediately. Zeke has been through three women since I have been here, and one of them, Cynthia, who is not, I repeat, not, a student at Lady Brit, even moved in with us for several months and had the nerve to treat me as though I were their foster son adopted from the We-Are-the-World Foundation, or something.

The first *coupe de feu*, which is what Zeke called them, was Zinaida, the manic depressive from Grosse Pointe, Michigan. Zinaida's mother had stabbed the father with a carving knife at Thanksgiving dinner, and she was doing five years in the slammer for assault with a deadly weapon. Zinaida was into dance at Lady Brit, and after her mother's Jean Harris number, Zinaida's creative insincts grew wilder. She hitched up with Zeke, who says psycho-biology is his field of study, and she persuaded him to buy a boa constrictor that she could use in her dancing and that he could study. Of course, she's also into therapy now because this knifing thing and mother-behind-bars have driven her bonkers, and she and Zeke spend hours together talking and drinking.

The next thing I knew, the damn snake had vanished and students all over the dorm were complaining because little kittens and even whole cats began disappearing one-by-one, and people were hearing strange noises at night in the walls and ceilings. Needless to say, old intrepid Director of Student Housing, not to mention the Dean, was not amused, and both Zeke and I got chewed out and threatened with expulsion. I think it would have happened if I hadn't thrown a crying jag in the Dean's office because of the unfairness of it all. I mean, why should I be dragged through the astroturf because of Zeke's smarmy affair with this demented Zinaida?

Finally, they called in an Orkin man who pulled the damn snake out of the wall, and so everybody calmed down. I am sure my act did the job, but Zeke says his mother was really the prime mover. Maybe so. She has enough pull around here.

After the snake incident, the Zinaida shebang didn't last much longer. She had just had her nose pierced; Zeke gave her a diamond from South Africa to put into her nose; but the two of them got into one awful fight one night in the parking lot. She slammed the door on his hand and broke it, but he hauled off with his other hand and gave her a black eye. She was so upset that she had to take a term off and shag back to Grosse Pointe where, I gather, her problems were less fearsome.

Then came Cynthia--"K-Mart Kitty"--I called her because that's actually where Zeke met her. For one who could afford Brooks Brothers and Saks Fifth, Zeke shopped in the damnedest places. He loved K-Mart for cheap flannel shirts and underwear, and so he met this little chippie who was selling them there. Then he had the nerve to bring her home to our place where he installed her into his room. And she starts tidying up the place, making little changes, like bringing in a microwave oven--you are not supposed to have them--and the next thing I know we are all playing house, and I am actually bopping around like some little Cosby kid.

That was Zeke's big taco period. Tacos were all Cynthia seemed to understand. She wasn't too bright, this one, and not blonde and vaguely Gaborish like Zinaida. Cynthia was brunette and dumpy and dumb, if you ask me.

Zeke's vocabulary changed during this period, also. Everything was "tacomundo" to him, or he would say, "I'm tacoed out," meaning he had eaten too many tacos or had had too much of life. When he was happy, he would blurt out "Amundo," meaning "wonderful," and he would pile us into his van which also doubled as a Dick Tracy-type portable garage for his motorcycle, and drive us all to exotic places like Brighton Beach or Wildwood, New Jersey, in search of better tacos, pizzas, chicks, or motorcycles, Zeke's passions at this time. And, actually, I felt that Cynthia had a calming influence on him, but the trouble was that he used to beat her up when he got angry, and she used to take it. She would leave for a while, but then come back, and sometimes she would talk to me about how mean Zeke was to her, and I would tell her to remember Robin Givens and I would say, "Did someone hurt Mommy again?" God, I was like something out of William Blake! A little song of innocence!

Zeke signed up for a Russian course at Lady Brit because he said Hannah, his grandmother, had been born in Russia and he wanted to learn a few dirty jokes in Russian to tell her; in his class he met his third flame, Tanya. Tanya was a beautiful brunette communist from New Orleans. I think she was sent to Lady Brit by the ghosts of Lenin and Stalin to work on fools like Zeke.

While she was busy proselytizing him, he was busy seducing and using her. Up to now, he had been coasting along in his studies, but now the crunch was coming and

Zeke knew it, so he took advantage of the crusading spirit in Tanya to make himself her chief cause.

Tanya discovered two things about Zeke. One, he had Hodgkin's disease, or claimed it, and told her about it. He called it "my reality" and added, "Reality must be learned." Everything revolved around the date when he learned he had this disease. "Oh, that was before Reality," he would say, or "After Reality."

The second thing she learned is that he was severely dyslexic and had successfully resisted all attempts to help him, out of pride or whatever. "All I want," Zeke said, "is to shovel in the information now." He was very bright and quick, but since much of any student's work at Lady Brit had to be put into writing, Zeke couldn't make it without a translator. So Tanya became his human computer, working with him on his animal experiments and zapping the whole thing into intelligible words for him so that he could pass his courses and graduate. She did all this at peril to her own studies in Russian literature.

"It's a scam not getting toasted anymore," Zeke complained to me one rainy afternoon.

"If you ask me, it's just as well you are not drinking anything these days."

"I've got this big do on my rat project to hand in."

"Are you giving Tanya credit as co-author?"

"Don't be Bobby, Bitchy," he says. "She loves me, chile."

"Tell that to Mother Cynthia," said I.

"I'm on twofers," he replies. "I'm poetry in action."

"You sure are," I said, hammering out on the computer for him to see, "To an Athlete Dying Young."

Zeke looked over my shoulder. "Only on weekends," he said. "Sometimes the quick squish appeals to me."

"Good luck on your project," I said. "Someday it will be nice to have the boa constrictor, the piranhas, the other fish, the mice, the rats, the hamster, and the women out of this place."

"Bobby, baby," he says to me. "Don't you like living in a pet shop?"

"Zeke, do me one big favor, please? Just do step outside and don't come back for a long, long time."

Zeke and Tanya on rats and aggression. God, I could win a Nobel Prize with what I know. Zeke bought this huge aquarium and filled it with cedar chips at the bottom. He came waltzing in one day with three ugly rats, and then he and Tanya actually spent the entire morning dying the rats' hairs with food coloring. One was red, another was yellow, and the third was green. "The three punkettes," Zeke called them.

They had these various categories for the poor rats. Closed-handled meant crowded conditions; human gloved-hand meant fondling, petting, or stroking. Open-unhandled meant uncrowded and not touched by human hands, and so on.

Believe it or not, what Zeke was watching was the rats' rate of urination. One rat, which was in the open-unhandled category, urinated in fifteen seconds. Tanya recorded all this vital information in a notebook. "R" for "red" rat urinated in fifteen seconds, "G" for "green" rat urinated in nineteen seconds, and "Y" for "yellow" rat urinated in twenty-two seconds. I remember this example well because I shouted out, "Send that info to the Guinness Book of Records!"

After urinations, they recorded defecations. Can you imagine living in the middle of all this and keeping a straight face? They started watching each little shit the rats took, Tanya solemnly recording it in Zeke's book. "The yellow rat shat at 8:02 p.m. The red rat took a dump at 10:22." Great moments in Literature, let me tell you!

Then they had a whole period when they were watching "Aggressive Activity." They would sit for hours observing the rats attack one another and mark down the exact time and all. I told them there was a war that came and went in Iraq, but they never even noticed.

Tanya also entered into the log "Social Interaction." This included such goodies as face washing, fur fluffing, mounting, and making little chattering noises. And, of course, every day was also feeding time at this zoo. When I think of what I had to put up with! Zeke would feed pinkies to the piranhas or snakes. These were baby mice or rats without hair. And, sometimes, he would throw them fuzzies, which were the same but with hair. Oscar, the big fish, always got tube effects, which were these dreadful sewage worms that Zeke bought in God knows what hell hole of a pet shop. Sometimes he talked about opening a pet shop himself or becoming a vet, and I encouraged this. I mean, when you can't really read or write, what are you going to do?

"Look at that," Zeke would say. "The rats sit around making bacon." That meant they were having babies. Zeke was fascinated with the whole process. He was like some diabolical god in this strange world. But he really did know a lot.

Tanya and Cynthia? There was a detente there, I guess. Usually, Cynthia was out slaving away at the old K-Mart when Tanya was doing her reform ministry among the disadvantaged over-privileged, so we never had an Annie Oakley-Calamity Jane set-to on the old frontier.

But, finally, after three terms had gone by and nothing had been done, I went to the Director of Student Housing, and, I mean, I simply had to spill my guts to him. I just hit him with everything I had. I said, "Do you know that there have been an increasing number of out-of-town tourists knocking on my door asking if we are the Western Connecticut zoo?" I told him, "If you want persons of my minority enrolling in your dubious little college and reflecting credit, not to mention money, on you in later years, you had better find me a new roommate and more attractive quarters *muy pronto.*"

To my surprise, he did. He found me a lovely little single which I repainted in my favorite colors, cerise and periwinkle blue. The room overlooks a pretty little rose garden that reminds me of Santa Monica. Nobody ever goes into this garden, so I have it all to myself.

I see Zeke and Tanya only rarely. Cynthia left, of course, after the Director of Student Housing realized she was living here like the Duchess of Windsor free of charge, and I believe Zeke has been banned completely on campus and is forced to live in town somewhere.

I am sure Tanya will pull Zeke through Lady Brit somehow, but I am really trying to put both of them out of my mind completely. There are just too many losers in this world as it is. I have decided I don't want to be one of them.

I'm sorry to say it, but I'm siding with Lewis Farrakhan and Johnnie Cochran from this point on. That's my project for this term: to survive. When and if I do, I'll have lots more to say that will interest Mr. Charlie Rose is a rose is a rose when he interviews me on his show.

Roger Lee Kenvin is the author of five collections of short
stories and a play published in India. His stories have been
published in literary magazines in the United States, Canada,
and England.